DATING MY BEST FRIEND

A SECOND CHANCE ROMANCE

ANNIE J. ROSE

A Second Chance at First Love.

It's been over a decade since tragedy ripped us apart.
We were just teens, but I never got to tell her I loved her.
Now I'm back in town, and Khloe doesn't want to see me.
Seconds after I walk into her work
I feel the same hot rush of longing I did all those years ago.
I still want her.
But there are secrets in the way.
I'm not the boy I was.
I'm a broken man with demons that chased me back from the
Marines.
She's still hurt that I broke my promise.
There's no room in her life for me now.
But this attraction won't be ignored.
Her lush mouth, her touch, they bring light to my dark
corners
But my secrets, my past, threaten to scare her off.
I don't know if she can handle what I've become.

I do know I can't stand to lose her again.
Not when I'd do anything to keep her.

CHAPTER 1

KHLOE - TWELVE YEARS AGO

"I got it, I got it, I got it."

"Yeah!"

"Shit."

The coach blew his whistle. "Language, Benson."

I raised my hand. "Sorry, Coach."

"Don't be sorry. Be better. All right, reset, and start again. Go!"

I jumped up and let the volleyball hit the pad of my forearm. All of us scrambled around the court, our tennis shoes squeaking and echoing off the walls. High school volleyball was competitive. I never came out of a game without a bruise or three on my body. I enjoyed the soreness, though. The aching of my muscles. The sports massages I knew my mother paid out of her ears to get me. I wanted to play in college in a school on the West Coast. That's where my heart was—volleyball and computer science.

Cal Tech was where I wanted to be.

The coach's whistle pierced the air, and we all stopped. I caught the ball and dropped back down to my feet, feeling my knees weakening. I was exhausted. Practices had been brutal to shake off the summer's laziness. But this was my senior year. I was freshly eighteen and ready to take on life. As I tucked the ball underneath my arm, I turned to see what was up.

Then, my mother's face came into view.

She and my coach were talking, but I didn't know what she was saying. It didn't look good, though, based on her expression. I tossed the ball to one of my teammates and jogged over, trying to figure out what they were talking about. The look on her face wasn't good—her brow furrowed deeper with every word, and the heat of her cheeks flushed all the way down her neck. She clutched the straps of her purse until her hand turned white.

"Mom? What's up?" I asked.

"Sweetheart, grab your bag. We have to go," she said.

Noting the tone of her voice, I darted into the locker room without question. I didn't look to my coach for approval. I didn't question what she said. My heart thundered in my chest as my shoes pounded the waxed floor. I burst through the doors of the locker room as panic filled my veins, my eyes searching for my bags.

I couldn't remember where I put my bags.

"The corner. By the window. I'll get your practice ball."

"Khloe, you got everything?"

"You good?"

"Here, your towel. Take it with you. Coach won't mind."

I caught the towel midair as I slung my bag over my shoulder. My teammates helped me track down all of my things as I wiped the sweat off my brow. I tossed the towel around my neck as one of the girls passed my ball to me. After catching it with one hand, I took one last look around the room, then rushed out to Mom.

I shot a look at the coach, who was chewing on the inside of his cheek. I furrowed my brow as he turned his back to me, his hand gravitating to his face. His neck turned a bright shade of red. The girls gathered around him as Mom took my hand. She practically dragged me out of the gym, and I knew then and there my life wouldn't ever be the same.

I just had to figure out why.

"Mom, what's going on?" I asked.

"We'll talk in the car, honey. Just come on. We have to hurry."

But we didn't talk in the car. Even though I asked her question after question, she didn't answer any of them. She just kept white-knuckling the steering wheel, speeding through yellow lights, and rolling stop signs as if they were mere suggestions while grinding her teeth together.

She always did that whenever she was worried.

"Mom, you're scaring me," I said.

"I don't mean to. Just sit tight."

"You said we'd talk. Why aren't you answering my questions?"

"Because I don't have a lot of answers right now, honey."

Tears rushed to my eyes. "What does that mean?"

She shook her head, and I watched her own eyes fill with tears. But when we pulled into the hospital, my thundering heart stopped in my chest. Why were we here? Why were we parking? She motioned for me to get out, and I dropped everything at my feet. I scrambled out of the car, slamming the door behind me. Mom reached for my hand, and I jogged beside her, eventually pulling her through the hospital doors.

"Your father's already here with Quinn. Jasper's been waiting for you. Come on, we have to hurry."

"Mom, tell me what's going on," I said.

I ripped my hand from her, and we stopped in the middle of the hallway.

"Honey, we have to get to the waiting room."

"Answer my question, Mom. Now. Why are we at the hospital? Why is Jasper here?" I asked.

She sighed. "There's been an accident."

Her words stopped me in my tracks. If Dad and Quinn were here, then it wasn't our family. Which meant…

"Come on. We have to go," I said.

I ran past my mother and left her in my dust. I blazed a trail down the hallway, slamming through doors and following the signs to the emergency waiting room. I came to a grinding halt when I saw them sitting there—Dad, with tears in his eyes, holding Quinn, who was openly sobbing. But as Mom jogged up behind me, trying to catch her breath, my eyes fell to Jasper. My best friend. My confidant.

Looking like an empty carcass.

"Oh, no," I whispered.

I slowly walked over and sat down in the empty seat next to Jasper, and he slowly moved his gaze to meet mine. His dead stare ingrained itself into my memory. I knew I'd never forget it. Not in a million years. And as tears slipped from his eyes, I felt mine fall in return.

"Hey, Jay," I whispered.

His face wrinkled up, and his head fell against my shoulder. I buried my face into his thick head of hair as I wrapped my arms around him. Tears fell against his scalp. I pulled him as close as I could get him, and as Mom sat down on the other side of Quinn, I rocked us side to side.

"It's okay. I'm here," I whispered.

I didn't dare bombard him with questions. Not now. I knew it was worse than I could have ever imagined. I knew something terrible had happened. Something life-altering.

Where were Jasper's parents?

I looked around the room, searching for answers. I held the boy I loved as I tried desperately to figure out how to fix this. Jasper was everything to me. My best friend. My neighbor from up the road. I confided in him about every little thing. Late-night phone calls were our specialty, and Saturdays were reserved for movie marathons at his place.

"Where are your parents, Jay?" I whispered.

"There's—there's been a-a-a-a—a wreck."

He stuttered out the words just as a nurse approached us. My eyes slowly scaled her body, and she seemed monumental in proportion to us. She squatted down and placed her knee against Jasper's. He lifted his head from my shoulder and wiped the tears from his eyes. He took my hand, our fingers threaded together. And as I held the hand of the boy I loved, I watched his soul break behind his eyes at the nurse's voice.

"I'm so sorry, Jasper. But there isn't anything we could do."

The piercing wail that left his lips shattered my heart. My face wrinkled up as he bent forward in his chair. His face turned red with his unearthly sound as he unleashed all of the pain of his heart through his mouth. Mom got up and tried to comfort him. Dad took his other hand. Quinn started crying harder as I got to my feet, scooting between his body and the nurse. I felt like I needed to shield him.

"Up. Come on. Get up, Jay."

I wrapped my arms around his body. I held him close as his dead weight seated against me. With my legs wobbling from practice, I dug down deep into the pit of my body, deep into the marrow of my bones. I pulled forth a strength I didn't know I had within me, and as my best friend yelled against my shoulder, I cried against his.

"No, please. Wake me up, Khloe."

I wanted to sell my soul to Satan. I wanted to give up my place in heaven to bring his parents back. As he clung to me, soaking my practice jersey, I drew in shallow breaths. Dad rubbed his back. Mom kept kissing the side of his head.

Quinn wrapped her little arms around Jay's waist, and I pressed myself as close to his quaking body as I could.

"I'm right here. I've got you, Jay. I've got you."

I felt helpless and pathetic. When I felt someone's hand come down against my shoulder. I shrugged them off. I felt the hand again. And again. And when I felt it for the third time, I craned my neck back.

"Cut it out," I hissed.

"Honey, it's the doctor. Let Jay speak to the doctor," Mom said.

Mom held me back as the doctor pulled him off to the side. Dad took my hand, keeping me from pulling away from Mom. I couldn't hear much, but I heard enough. Neither of Jay's parents made it out of that crash.

I saw the doctor motion for someone, and a staunch, paunchy man wearing a police uniform got up. I strained against my parents' arms as my little sister kept crying.

The doctor looked up and motioned for me. With what strength I had left, I pulled away from my parents. I rushed to Jay and wrapped my arms around him, feeling his wing-span descend around me. I placed my head against his shoulder and felt him settle his cheek on top of my head. And as silent tears streaked my cheeks, I listened to the police officer walk us through what was next.

"What happens to me, sir?" Jay asked.

"Well, you're not quite eighteen yet, son. So, we have to find your next of kin. That's the first step," the officer said.

"What, like, grandparents?"

"Yes. Do you have any grandparents around here?"

I shook my head. "They died when he was pretty young."

Jay nodded. "Yeah."

The officer sighed. "All right. Any aunts? Uncles? Older cousins around here?"

"I mean, not around here. But—"

"Where do they live?"

I furrowed my brow. "Why does that matter?"

The officer licked his lips. "Because until he turns eighteen, he has to be in the presence of a legal adult. A legal guardian. So, wherever his closest relative is—"

"That's where I'm moving," Jay finished.

My head snapped up. "No."

"He doesn't have a choice. It's the law."

I looked up at him. "This is not okay. Your aunt lives in Vegas. All the way in Vegas, Jay."

The officer sighed. "Do you have anyone that lives any closer than that?"

When Jay slowly shook his head, I knew this night was about to get infinitely worse.

CHAPTER 2

JASPER

Khloe was silent as we packed up my things, which wasn't like her at all. But I couldn't blame her for being upset. I kept stealing glances at her, taking in her auburn hair and her sad brown eyes.

This past week had been hard on all of us. The Bensons had kindly taken me in while the police attempted to track down my aunt, an old woman I'd only met twice that lived all the way in Las Vegas. She was odd. Eccentric. That much I remembered about her. She was my father's estranged sister, and why the two of them didn't talk, I didn't have a clue. The police had such a hard time tracking her down because she'd apparently been in the Bahamas for the past two weeks, participating in relief efforts from hurricane season, of all things.

At least she's generous.

"Are you okay?"

Khloe's voice pierced my thoughts, and I slowly stood up. I gazed around my bedroom, looking at all the pictures on the wall. The pictures on my night table that I had to place facedown because I couldn't bear to look at my parents' faces. My lower lip quivered. I had cried so much this past week, I thought I might drown. Surely, death was sweeter than this pain and emptiness I felt.

"Uh, no, Khlo. really not okay."

I felt her arms wrap around my waist, but I pulled away from her. Her touch hurt too much. After losing my parents in some heinous accident, I'd lose her too. Khloe. The girl I loved. The girl who always teased me about being just a few months older. The girl I always called at midnight just to see what she was up to. The girl I spent every Saturday with ever since we were in middle school together, fighting off bullies who teased her over her glasses. I'd coaxed her through the pain in her mouth whenever she got her braces tightened and cried with her when she lost her pet gerbil at the hands of her little sister who let it out the back door of their home to play.

I was losing everything that mattered most to me.

And I certainly wasn't okay with it.

"I'm sorry," she whispered.

I shook my head. "Not your fault."

"Are you packing up everything, or…?"

"I mean, take what you want if that's what you're asking."

"That's not what I'm asking. I just don't know if you're leaving anything behind."

The bite of her voice made me sigh. We'd been fighting a lot this past week. And the two of us never fought. We discussed, sure. Argued, maybe. But fighting? No, we never did that. It hurt me to argue with her, too. I knew she was trying to help. I knew she was trying to make the best of our limited time together. But I wasn't in the mood for movie marathons and late-night discussions and talks on the back porch.

All I wanted to do was rewind time.

I blinked back my tears and walked over to my closet. I

kept my back to Khloe, hoping that I would finally wake up from this nightmare. But the more I folded up my clothes, the more it sank in.

My parents were dead.

I was leaving for Las Vegas tomorrow.

And I'd never see Khloe again.

Over the past few days, I'd wanted to tell her. I'd wanted to pour my heart out to her and tell her about the exact moment when I fell in love with her. I wanted to take her in my arms, kiss her for the first time, and tell her that I'd be coming back for her. That way, when I graduated from whatever school I'd be going to in Vegas, I'd come all the way back to Connecticut to get her, no matter what it took. Hearing her sniffle broke my heart. I stole glances over my shoulder at her and saw her shoulders shaking.

"I'm sorry. I'm just—"

She shook her head. "No, no. It's okay."

"Khlo, you don't have t—"

"I'll start packing up your bathroom."

"Khlo, stop."

She paused her movements, but she didn't turn around.

"Look at me," I said.

When she didn't move, I walked over to her.

I set my hands on her shoulders and turned her around to face me. Her gaze sat heavily against my chest, and I crooked my finger underneath her chin. Her eyes met mine, and I gazed into those beautiful brown orbs. When those green flakes in her eyes came to life, it reminded me of Christmas, my favorite time of year.

The Christmas we wouldn't spend together this year.

I love you. Say it.

No. That would hurt her more.

Then, kiss her. Leave her with something.

And then what? Tell her to wait for me?

You have to do something.

"Jay?" she asked softly.

I gripped her chin. "You're my best friend. And no matter where I go, that will never change. Okay?"

She blinked. "Okay."

"When I get to my aunt's place, the first thing I'm doing is calling."

Tears rushed to her eyes. "Okay."

"And we'll still do our late-night calls. And watch movies together over the phone. Okay?"

She paused, almost as if she didn't believe me, and that broke my heart.

"Okay," she whispered.

"Come here," I murmured.

I wrapped Khloe up in my arms and sighed. I felt her crying against my chest, and I did my best to be strong for her. The funeral had been yesterday, and things had been hard on all of us. The reception felt empty. The laughter felt stale. Even remembering my parents with stories felt trite and contrived. Nothing felt the same. Nothing felt good anymore. And as Khloe collapsed in my arms, I dragged her over to the bed.

"Come on. It's okay. I promise," I whispered.

She curled against me, and I cursed myself. I cursed how good it felt. I cursed my want to stay behind with her. Why the fuck did this have to happen now? I mean, I'd be eighteen in January. Couldn't my aunt just come hang out up here until my birthday? That was only four-ish months. It could be another vacation for her.

A shadow moving out in the hallway caught my eye. I looked over toward the door and saw Mrs. Benson slowly come into view. She tossed me a sad smile before coming in. She sat down next to me on the bed and pulled her daughter into her lap. Khloe fought her mother, but her mother didn't give in. When Khloe finally collapsed against her, I got up and turned my back.

I was jealous of the fact that her parents were still alive.

It hurt to be in this house. To smell my mother's perfume and walk by my father's cigar room. My mother had hated that room. It always clouded up the hallway, she'd said. But over the past couple of days, I had immersed myself in that room, drawing in the smoke-tainted air through my nostrils. I let myself sit in his chair and curl up against his robe. Hell, I even plucked one of his Cubans from the glass container and lit it up myself, coughing and hacking my way through the first five puffs before breaking down and crying.

How am I going to empty this house out?

How was I supposed to know how to do any of this? I owed the Bensons everything. Not just for taking me in this past week, but for helping me plan the funeral. Helping me pick out burial plots. Helping me with the payment for tombstones. I didn't know about any of that.

They had made so many phone calls on my behalf, it was sickening.

And I had no idea how I'd ever repay them for it.

Maybe there's a service I could hire to empty this house for me.

I packed up what I could stand to take. I even stole a few things from my father's cigar room. Mainly his collection. I didn't want to smoke them, but I wanted to light them up and smell him again. I took his white-gold lighter and the butane fluid for it. I packed up his smoke-laden robe and stole a few books from my mother's library that I could stand to look at. Maybe I'd have the service pack up some of these things and put them in storage, at least until I could go through them and figure out what I wanted to keep.

But until then, this was all I could manage to touch.

I closed the front door behind me and gave one last look at my house before heading down the block with Khloe and

Mrs. Benson. Once there, I locked myself in their spare room and didn't come out for the rest of the night.

"Want some cocoa?"

Quinn's voice woke me from a dead sleep. She stood looking down at me, holding a cup of steaming liquid.

I nodded slowly. "Sure. Yeah."

I got out of bed and followed her down the hall to the living room, where I sat on the couch.

It was scorching outside. This summer had been the hottest on Connecticut's record, but I didn't care. I mindlessly sipped the chocolate drink and gazed out the living room window. I leaned over, staring down the street and getting a glimpse of the corner of my parents' house.

"Quinn?" I asked.

"Yeah!" she called from the kitchen.

"Is Khlo here?"

"No, she went back to school."

Quinn sat down on the couch with me, curling up with her hot cocoa. She started sweating, the damn drink was so hot. The television droned on with some sort of commercial. I furrowed my brow as I looked down into my drink.

"Why aren't you at school right now?" I asked.

"I faked being sick so I could stay home."

"Ah."

"Figured you could use the company."

My heart warmed at her words. "Thanks, kiddo."

"Uh-huh."

She laughed along with the TV, and the sound didn't grate against my ears. I didn't watch the television, but I did get a kick out of her laughter. Quinn always snorted after she laughed. Like, really laughed. It was honestly cute. And Khloe had the same quirk about her.

Though, it was immensely cuter on Khloe.

"She's going to miss you."

Quinn's voice pierced my haze. "What?"

"Khloe. She's going to miss you."

I sighed. "I'm going to miss her, too."

"Promise to call, right?"

"Oh, yes."

"And come back to visit?"

"I only have to finish my senior year. Then, I'm free to do as I wish, apparently."

"Good. Because we're all going to miss you."

I wrapped my arm around her. "Really? You're gonna miss me, huh?"

She shrugged my arm off. "Not that much. But maybe a little bit."

"Oh, oh, yeah. Just a little bit."

She rolled her eyes. "Goofball."

I grinned. "Love ya, too, Q."

My eyes fell back out the window, and I sighed. I dreamed about what life might be like without Khloe only a few houses up from me. No more hanging out on the couch during rainy Saturdays watching old game shows. No more late-night back-porch conversations when her parents pissed her off. No more volleyball games to cheer relentlessly at just so I could embarrass her as much as possible.

No more seeing her in the bleachers at my basketball games.

A knock came at the door, and Quinn shot up. She raced for the door, sloshing her hot cocoa everywhere. I sighed as I set mine down. I figured whoever was at the door was probably there for me. I smoothed my hands over my shirt and tried to prepare myself. But when Quinn opened the door, I really wasn't prepared at all.

An older woman with white streaks in her dark brown hair stood there. She looked at me and nodded, then beckoned with her head to come on. I almost didn't recognize her. But I did recognize the beauty mark on her chin. Those thin fish lips my father had. And she had my father's eyes.

"Aunt Maybelle?" I asked.

"Come on. We have to head out," she said.

I blinked. "But I'm not—I'm not ready. I'm not fully packed."

"I know. I went to the house. I'll help you with the rest. But we have to get your stuff to the airport. Our flight leaves at six."

"So soon?"

"I have to get back home before I have to go back to work."

"Mom!" Quinn exclaimed.

I winced at her voice. "I'm not ready to leave yet."

My aunt sighed. "And I wasn't ready to bury my brother. But we all have to do things we aren't ready for. I might be able to buy another day off work. But that still doesn't change the fact that I can't move our flights. I've already moved them twice to give you some room."

I heard Mrs. Benson rushing down the stairs, and Quinn started talking at lightning speed. As I stood there, staring at this strange woman I was supposed to go with, my only thought was of Khloe.

I couldn't leave without seeing her. Without hugging her. Without telling her goodbye.

She'd never forgive me for that if I did.

CHAPTER 3

KHLOE - PRESENT DAY

My glasses slid down my nose as I fiddled with my keys. Curses fell from my lips as my bag slid down my shoulder, and my coffee dripped over my knuckles; the sweetened black liquid almost wasted. I finally got my key into the door and kicked it open, my heel clinking against the metal door.

"Come on. Get inside," I murmured to myself.

I sighed as the door banged closed behind me. The darkness of the backroom had become an all too familiar sight. I knew where everything was, despite not being able to see it, but as my legs carried me over to the light switch, I felt my shin slam against something.

"Shit," I hissed in pain.

Okay. Maybe not everything. But still.

Six years ago, no one would have ever convinced me that the library would've been my domain to control. And not only that, but I would've laughed at them had they told me it would become my safe space. I'd hated reading as a girl. Sports were my thing. Volleyball, especially. But things change. People change. They grow, and they morph. They're formed by their experiences. And me? Well, I was a product of the life I had lived.

The solitary life I had chosen for myself.

I flipped on the light switch and let out a relieved sigh. I glanced around the room before looking down, taking stock of the metal cart that had gotten in my way. The new hire, no doubt. Part-time punk high school kid who didn't give a shit about books or how we filed things away or where things were supposed to go.

I kicked the cart into its designated corner before dropping my bag to the floor.

"All right. Much better," I said breathlessly.

My coffee traded hands before I shook my soaked knuckles. At least a fourth of my coffee had spilled over the edge of my cheap thermos. All the more reason to get a new one, I supposed. And with my newest promotion to full-time head librarian, I'd surely have the money to get one now.

I've made it, John. I'm doing okay. I missed him. I missed him more than I could stand. But time always healed wounds. That much I knew. His funeral had been hard. Sitting there, with my back straight, watching his family next to me weep and cry and find solace against my shoulder. The funeral had been an absolute nightmare. Planning his last vigil here on this planet had sucked the life out of me. His heart attack had taken everyone by surprise since he had been such an avid runner.

I missed my late husband more than I could stand sometimes.

But it didn't hurt anymore.

And that was something.

John's funeral had been three years ago. When my mother called me and told me to get to the hospital as soon as possible, it was as if I had been reliving a nightmare—something that felt all too familiar. I knew the second I walked through those emergency room doors that it wasn't good. I knew the second I looked into my mother's face that my life would, once again, be altered permanently. That I would, yet again, lose someone I had given my heart, my soul, and the promise of my world to.

My lower lip quivered as I sipped my hot coffee.

These past three years had been long and hard. I had spent more and more time at the library as I grieved. It was the quiet place that I'd needed as I healed. And in that quiet space, I got to relive some of my greatest memories with John. I remembered our wedding all those years ago when I was only twenty and not quite out of college yet. I remembered all the vacations we took, jetting off to London for two weeks to see the Olympics live, or flying straight into Dallas as a late birthday gift to him to see the Super Bowl. John loved those charged events where everyone cheered and cursed as one.

"Khloe, you back here?"

Matt's voice pulled me from my thoughts as the door beside me opened.

"Hey. I thought I saw the light back here. What time did you get in?"

I sipped my coffee. "Just a few minutes ago, actually. Do you have something to do this morning?"

He grinned. "Yep. A last-minute booking from the elementary school up the road. They want to bring the kids to hear a couple of stories and do crafts in the craft room. Apparently, it's supposed to snow today, which means they can't go to the petting zoo."

"Well, what fun for you."

He snickered. "It's really not that bad."

"A throng of jittery children sounds horrible. I don't know how you do it."

"Well, I love kids, for starters. And I've seen you around kids. You don't hate them."

I shrugged. "Yeah, I can tolerate them just fine."

"Ah, you don't give yourself enough credit."

"Do you have working hours today?"

"Do you not know, Miss Head Librarian?"

I sighed. "No, I haven't taken a look at the schedule for this week. Humor me, oh woeful employee."

He smiled softly. "I work until two, then I'm done until Thursday."

"Good to know."

Matt was the children's librarian, and usually, it was only the two of us. However, the library board—which was essentially the mayor and the family the library was dedicated to—released funds for the part-time employee I was very eager to fire. He hadn't been doing the best job. This was the fourth bruised shin I'd have. And this was after telling him where the cart belonged at the end of the day on six separate occasions. He didn't follow directions well, but Matt had a soft spot for the kid.

Well, all kids, actually.

So, I'd keep him around for another week or two. But if things didn't shape up, I had no issues firing a sixteen-year-old. This was my house now. It had to run like a well-oiled machine in order to save my sanity.

I shoved myself ass-first through the door that led out into the main lobby of the library. I walked across the small hall and slipped my key into the door. Unlocking it brought me great pride, especially now that it finally had my name on the door. I opened it with my hip and quickly caught the coffee sloshing over the edge of my thermos with my mouth.

But when I bent down to pick up my bag...

"Looking for this?"

Matt's voice emanated from behind me, and I slowly

turned my head with my lips puckered up to the thermos. He chuckled as he handed my bag off to me. I blushed furiously and took it from him. I nodded my thanks before slipping into my office, and after the door swung closed behind me, I leaned against it.

"All right, Khloe. You got this. Another dawn, another day."

While our library wasn't large in size, we serviced a three-town radius, which meant a lot of kids passed through our doors. Those kids and their elementary school trips easily justified Matt's position here. While I wasn't a fan of his working hours, him preferring to work weekends was the reason why I got them off. Mostly. So, I tried not to complain too much. Though, the field trips always kept me locked up in my office unless I had to come out and speak.

I'd never been a big fan of small children.

They were grimy and sticky and bratty and spoiled. No one raised their kids to be respectful these days. I had been thankful that John hadn't wanted kids. Especially since his sudden death would have left me a single mother.

I walked over to my computer and started it up, then I sat in my chair and sipped my coffee, trying my best not to waste any more of it.

"All right. Let's see what you have for me today."

I started sifting through the system, checking for any loans or overdue fees that needed to be collected. We had an electric scanner built into the side of the building, capable of scanning books as they came through. It didn't automatically scan them back in, but it captured pictures of the title so I could rifle through them and enter them into the system. Not a perfect system, but a little more convenient than the old days where everything was done by hand and took forever.

I set up the system to send out automatic notices to all of

those who had overdue fees. I double-checked those who had paid theirs against the system to make sure no one called to get angry with me. Then, I checked in the books. The library was empty for the first hour, usually, which meant I had time to toggle books in before going to put them away on the shelves. I enjoyed my empty mornings in the library.

A knock came at my door.

"Yes, Matt?"

My door inched open. "Want me to get started on the books?"

I nodded. "That'd be nice, yes. There are more overdue fees than usual. I have to send more notices out."

He nodded. "Um, there's actually someone out here to see you."

I raised my gaze to his. "Oh?"

"Yeah. Someone in a police cruiser? Said it's urgent."

I grinned. "Get started on those books. I'll handle it."

I tapped away on my computer for a few more minutes before I pushed away from my desk. I rushed out of my office and barreled through the automatic doors to see the cruiser parked at the curb. Kent crossed his arms over his chest as I approached him, but my feet quickly slowed their pace. Even though I smiled at him, he didn't smile back.

And my gut curled in on itself.

"What is it?" I asked.

"Morning, Khloe."

"What's wrong, Kent?"

He sighed.

"I just caught wind of something I figured you'd wanna know."

"Well, can you spit it out? I'm kind of getting my workday off the ground."

He licked his lips. "I figured you'd wanna—well, you see—"

"Spit it out or let me get back to my coffee."

"Jasper's back in town, Khloe."

I drew in a sharp breath of air. It felt like someone had punched me in the gut and stolen my breath.

"Are you sure?" I asked.

Kent nodded. "I knew you'd wanna know."

"Yeah, yeah. Uh, thank you for telling me. Have you seen him?"

"Yeah. I'm actually going to be training him here."

I blinked. "Are you serious?"

"Yeah." The thought of Jasper working with the Canaan Police Department was enough to throw me off balance. I teetered on my feet before I felt a pair of strong hands grip me, holding me steady as Kent's voice pierced through the haze.

"Come on. That's it, lean against the cruiser."

"Hey, you good, Khloe?"

I nodded. "Yeah, I just need a minute."

"You need me to call someone? Or get you something?"

"No," I said, standing up straight and taking in a breath. "No, I'm good. Thanks for letting me know. Stay safe, Kent."

I slipped away from Kent's hands and made my way back into the library. I felt him staring after me, but I didn't bother to look back. I had to get behind closed doors before I lost my shit.

"Khloe, you okay?" Matt asked.

"Get those books put up, please," I said.

Then, I locked myself in my office, hoping to bypass children's story time as tears streamed down my face.

CHAPTER 4

JASPER

I sat in the driveway of my parents' old house and sighed. My aunt had kept it in my name all these years, but sitting there, looking at my old front porch, still hurt. And I swear to fuck, I still smelled my father's cigars all the way out here. I closed my eyes and leaned back into the seat of my truck. I felt tired, so very tired, deep within the marrow of my bones.

I'm back in Canaan.

So much had happened over the past twelve years. I moved to Vegas. Graduated high school. Enlisted into the Marines and did my four years. Got out of the Marines and somehow carved out a police career for myself in Vegas, only to hate the lights and the smell of vomit and having to revive more people from drug overdoses than actually arrest people for doing shitty things on the Strip.

I don't know what the hell I was thinking, looking up jobs in Canaan. I hadn't been here in almost thirteen years. But when I saw the police department had an opening, I applied for it without hesitation.

Vegas never did feel like home.

Then again, Canaan didn't, either. Not since my parents passed away. My eyes fell open, and I stared at the garage door, wondering how the fuck to open it now.

I need to get the code reset.

I guess it was good that I had a place to sleep tonight. But my aunt never did have the courage to get the house cleaned out. There had been no estate sale. There had been nothing put in storage. The house got locked up, my aunt ordered courtesy patrols of the neighborhood, and she used my father's life insurance policy to have recurring flowers sent to their gravesites every Friday, rain or shine. She also paid to have the grass cut every week and the snow cleared when needed.

And my mother's life insurance? Well, she gave that to me. I'd promptly stuffed it away into investments to let it sit.

I opened my truck door and slid out onto the concrete. I closed the door behind me and looked around. The damn place hadn't changed in years. The houses still looked the same. The mailboxes hadn't changed in style. This driveway was still cracked and overgrown a bit with weeds, something I'd have to fix if I wanted to sell this place.

Do I want to sell this place?

"One step at a time," I murmured.

"What was that?"

I turned around at the sound of the voice. And the girl—no, woman—walking up the driveway made my jaw drop open. I almost choked at the sight of her. Holy hell, could it really be her?

"Quinn?" I asked.

She smiled. "Guess I don't look that different, huh?"

I shook my head. "You've grown."

"That's what happens after more than a decade."

"You look…"

Just like your sister.

"Like a woman instead of the girl who guzzled hot chocolate like it was her life force?"

I laughed. "Please tell me you still drink it."

She smiled. "Year-round, like always."

"Nice to know some things don't change."

Her stare fell down my body. "And yet, some things do. A lot."

I knew I looked different from the last time she'd seen me too. I'd gotten a bit taller, and being in the military had put some muscle on me. I had a couple of tattoos on my arms and chest after drunken nights out with the guys in my unit. My hair was probably disheveled, too. I'd driven straight from Vegas all the way to here once I caught wind of the fact that they'd offered me the position.

"I can't believe you're back."

Quinn's whisper hit my ears a little too hard. She'd always been a loud girl. Boisterous. A bit too "in your face." She didn't understand the idea of personal space. At least, when she was younger, she didn't. But now, as she stood near the bed of my truck and me near the driver's door, it seemed like she had gotten the hang of it.

Or, she was afraid to approach me.

Maybe because of Khlo?

Would Khloe even want me calling her that after what I'd done?

"I heard you were back from Kent and all. But I guess part of me didn't believe it," Quinn said.

"I recognize that name. Officer Blue?" I asked.

"Yeah. How do you know that?"

I sighed. "Just took a job with the police department. He's my training officer."

She laughed. "Well, fuck me. Small town, I guess."

"Yeah. Small town."

"Well, I figured I'd come over and surprise you. So, surprise."

She held out her arms, and I chuckled softly.

"You got me," I said.

Guess Officer Blue had a bit of a mouth on him. Because other than him, only the chief knew I was coming. I guess it didn't help that the chief used to be good buddies with my father. I probably got the job more off that than anything else. But I was a good cop. I had a proven track record back in Vegas. If anyone doubted me, they could take a look at my record.

But how did Quinn know I was showing up today?

"You look like a deer in headlights. You okay?" Quinn asked.

"How did you know I was coming in today?" I asked.

"Word travels fast around here. Especially when a long-lost soul comes back to town."

I winced at her words. "I guess, yeah."

I heard my dog whimpering in the front seat, and I was grateful for the way out of that particular conversation.

"Gotta get Piper, hold on," I murmured.

I wrapped around the front of the truck, trying to keep as much distance between Quinn and me as possible. I didn't know why, but I was suddenly uncomfortable around her. But when I let my beautiful golden retriever out of the truck, personal space went out the window.

"Oh, my gosh!" Quinn squealed.

Piper jumped from her seat, and Quinn was at my side. She held her hand out, cooing to my dog as she sniffed Quinn's hand. She gasped and squealed at such a high pitch that it kicked up other dogs in the neighborhood. Their barking started Piper barking. And her tail wagged the more Quinn petted her. I rolled my eyes as the chorus of dogs kicked up, forcing their owners out to their backyards.

Quinn let Piper lick her face as I walked around to the bed of the truck. I reached in and pulled out my duffel bags, tossing both of them over my shoulders. Everything else could wait. I didn't have to unload immediately. Especially since I wasn't sure I'd want to be staying in my childhood home for very long.

There were too many painful memories here. "Need any help?" Quinn asked.

I ignored her question as I stepped onto the porch.

"Jasper, you need help?" she asked again.

I dropped my bags and fished around for my keys.

"All right. I'm just going to grab this, well, box here. Okay?" she asked.

I slid my key into the lock and turned. The door eased open with a creek, and the smell of my memories came wafting back. I swore I heard my mother laughing and smelled my father's fucking cigars. I closed my eyes and drew in a deep breath, forcing myself to take it all in. When Quinn stepped up behind me on the porch, I reached for my bags before stepping through the threshold.

Quinn coughed. "Think this place needs some dusting."

I ignored her words as I opened my eyes.

"And maybe some mopping, too. Has anyone been in here over the years?" she asked.

I wanted her to leave, but I didn't want to be rude. I knew my presence back would be jarring for a lot of people. Her sister, especially. So, I let Quinn ramble on in that style of hers that apparently hadn't changed with time.

But I sighed with relief when I flipped on the hallway light.

"Huh. Got the power turned on. Nice. Let me check the water."

Quinn rushed by me, and I dropped my bags again. I hadn't stepped foot in this house for damn near thirteen years. And yet, it hadn't changed one bit. It felt weird being back. It felt...off.

Oddly anticlimactic.

Thank fuck for that.

I reached behind me and closed the door. I heard water running in the distance and nodded my head. Good. Electricity and water meant a hot shower tonight. I turned toward the stairs. My eyes flitted across the pictures, refusing to take them in. And as Quinn started cooing at my dog again somewhere in the house, I walked over to the steps and began climbing.

One by one, they groaned underneath my feet. The carpet kicked up more dust than I could have imagined. But the smells of home slowly took me back to a time where Khlo and I had run through these hallways before falling onto the couches together to watch movies. Memories of Mom tucking me in at night, of Dad smoking in his cigar room and reading books to me through the door. He always knew I was sitting out there, listening, waiting for him to emerge.

I stopped just shy of that cigar room door and sat down, leaning my head against the wall like I always had when I was a kid.

Waiting to hear his voice.

He's not coming back, you idiot.

"I know, I know," I murmured.

You have to move on.

"I can't," I whispered.

You're a damn Marine! Oorah!

"Shut up," I growled to myself.

"You say something?" Quinn shouted up the stairs.

"Quinn, I don't mean to be rude, but—"

"It's okay. I know. I gotta jet anyway. Work, and all that. I just stopped by on my lunch break to say welcome home. But you should stop in some time and see the folks. They've missed you," she said.

I stood up. "Yeah. Sure. I'll make sure to get over there."

There was a heavy pause before she spoke again; this time, her voice much quieter. "She's missed you, too, Jasper. And she's been through a lot the past few years. You should go see her at the library."

I paused. "The library?"

"Yeah, here in town. Listen, I've gotta run. I'm about to be late for my shift. Welcome home, Jasper."

Then, my front door closed, leaving me alone with my dog and all sorts of questions running through my head.

"The library?" I whispered.

I stared at the staircase, wondering if I had the guts to actually stop by the town library and see if Khloe was there. My Khloe. Well, she wasn't mine. Never had been. Not since I left. Not since I never looked back even after promising that the only thing that would change between us was distance and only for a year.

Guilt barreled over me, and I turned my head away from the stairs. I pressed on until I stood in the doorway of my childhood room. I opened the door and peered inside. The damn thing looked the exact same way it had all those years ago. Memories came to life before my very eyes. Memories of Khloe and me lying on my bed and staring at the ceiling, laughing and talking and stressing over exams. I saw her with her head on my shoulder, crying like she had that day, holding me while I stared blankly at the wall.

Wishing all of it had been a nightmare.

Why the hell is she at the library? She's supposed to be in California being the next Bill Gates or some shit.

My head slowly panned around, and the large double doors came into view. The shadows of the hallway taunted me as the hallway grew longer and shorter in my vision. I felt sick to my stomach. After all these years, those doors still made me ache as much as I did that afternoon in the hospital.

But I didn't cry. Unlike all those years ago, I didn't even brew tears. I'd come to terms with it emotionally. Though, that hole would always be there. Every birthday. Every holiday. At the turn of every year. It was a painful reminder that more time had passed without them. More cigars were smoked before I could ever share one with my father. More books were read without my mother's whispered voice mouthing the words behind the back of my head.

More holidays passed without Khloe and me exchanging gifts like we always had.

You're an asshole, Jasper.

I'd left here and never called. I'd never offered an explanation for anything. I just…left. Like the grieving little coward that I was.

And now, I was back.

Hoping the girl I had hurt all those years ago didn't hate me now.

CHAPTER 5

KHLOE

"I hate him."

I growled the words as I slipped into my office. All damn day, people had been coming up to me, feeding me the news, asking me if I'd seen him. *Him.* Jasper Willem, the lost boy of Canaan. I leaned against my office door and closed my eyes. This place had been my solace all day until someone else came knocking. An old acquaintance from high school. The fucking FedEx guy, dropping off packages with new books to put on the shelves. Books donated by self-publishers who wanted to see their own titles on display.

A knock came at my door, and I drew in a deep breath. I ran my hands down my blouse, then quickly opened it. I put on my best smile and pushed my glasses up my nose, gazing into the stare of Jean Marine.

How her parents had to have loathed her presence to name her something like that.

"So, have you seen him?" she asked.

I blinked. "Are you here to pick up a book?"

She swatted me. "No, you silly goose. I saw him down at

the deli for lunch. Oh, he looks so much different! He's taller. Broader. I think the military did him some good."

I blinked again. "The library is for books, not gossip."

"Oh, come on. Don't tell me you're at least a little curious. I talked to him. You want all the details?"

"Matthew can help you behind the counter if you want to check out a book."

"Hey, wait a sec—Khloe!"

I closed the door in her face and threw the lock. I stalked over to my desk and flopped into my chair. I pulled my hair out from the clipped-up bun, then shook my tendrils out over my shoulders. I slid my hands down my face, tossed my glasses onto my desk, and sighed.

"Why did he have to come back?" I whispered.

More people came by to get a slice of that gossip pie than to actually check out a book. They were clogging up the library, making too much damn noise, and distracting me from my work. The library was my home. My sweet place of solace. And they were ruining it. Jasper was ruining it.

Maybe I needed to put a sign on the front of the library —"No, I haven't seen Jasper Willem!"—just so people would know without coming in and asking me. Because holy hell, I was tired of it. And I still had four more hours in my day.

Lord, help me through this day.

Another knock came at my door, and I bristled. I thought about not opening it and simply ignoring it. Turning off my office light. Closing my blinds. Hiding away from the world until my shift was over. But the knock came again, only this time more frantic.

So, I got up and answered the door.

"Yes, how can I—oh, hey, Matt."

He grinned. "So, have you seen him yet?"

My face fell, and I playfully swatted at him. He held up a hardback book to block my hand as I pretended to slap him.

He chuckled as a smile crossed my face. I was thankful for the moment of laughter.

"What's up?" I asked.

"I've got about an hour before it's time to go. Need anything done?" he asked.

"Just keep putting up books and trying to tame the rabid crowds. I'll be out by two to relieve you from front-desk duty."

"If you want, I can stick around until you close this place up."

"Nope. You're not slated to work a full day, so I'm not doing that to you."

"Want me to come by later, then? Help you close down? Bring you food? Set up a booth and pass out flyers telling people you haven't seen him yet?"

I grinned. "You know, that might be better than my idea to put up a sign on the front door."

He chuckled. "I bet we could find a neighborhood kid to spray-paint it on the outside of the library."

"I'm sure the city would love that."

He sighed. "Should I ask why his return is such a big deal?"

I shrugged. "The story is simple. We were best friends until his parents died. He left to live with his aunt in Vegas, and despite promises to the contrary, he never looked back. Not once."

He blinked. "That must have hurt."

Yeah, because I loved him. "It didn't feel good."

"How did his parents die?"

My mind rushed back to that moment. My mom pulling me from volleyball practice. Walking into the hospital waiting room. The way the nurse crouched down and delivered the news.

I cleared my throat. "Car accident."

"That's gotta be tough on a young boy."

"Yeah, well. It was tough on all of us."

Matthew grinned. "But you're not still bitter about it or anything, right?"

I waved him off. "I just don't like everyone coming in here and clogging up the place with long-forgotten gossip."

"At least it's been getting people into the library."

"Yeah? And how many books have been checked out?"

He paused. "Point taken."

I giggled. "Uh-huh. So, I'll come relieve you around—"

"Khloe!"

A few shushes rose up from the small crowd still in the library as my mother's voice bellowed through the front door.

"Khloe. You will never guess who I just talked to," Mom said.

Matthew clapped his hand over his mouth as I ground my teeth together.

"Jasper?" I asked.

"How did you know?"

"How could I not? It's not like this place is full of many newsworthy events," I grumbled.

"Well, he's been hired onto the police force," she said.

I blinked. "I thought he was in the military."

"You've talked to him?"

"No. But, the rest of the city apparently has and has made it a point to update me."

"Well, yes, he was in the Marines for four years. Got out, became a police officer. And oh, he looks so different. He's taller, I think. And very broad. He looks really handsome, too."

"Oh, I bet he does," Matthew said playfully.

I shot him a look. "Mom, please stop."

"Stop what?" She looked confused.

"Stop trying to play matchmaker."

She scoffed. "Come on. You know that's not what I'm trying to do. But he was your best friend for a long time," she said.

"How close were you?" Matthew asked.

"Don't you have a job to do?" I asked.

"Oh, don't be so hard on him. I'm sure he's just curious. Right, Michael?"

"Matthew," I said.

"Right, Matthew?" Mom corrected.

"Of course. Merely curious, that's all," he said, his eyes twinkling with mischief.

I glared at him, and he scurried back off to the front desk.

"Why are you so mean to him sometimes?" Mom asked.

"Can you get to the point, please?" I asked.

"Sweetheart, we all know Jasper Willem was your first love," she said.

"No, he wasn't."

"You can tell that to me all you want, but I remember those days. You two, paling around. How you looked at him. The way he looked at you. There's a reason Dad always kept an eye on you two whenever he came around."

"I didn't love him."

"You did. There's no point in denying it."

"Mom, what do you want? Because I'm kind of in the middle of work?"

Mom sighed. "At the very least, you owe it to yourself to get answers. Which will require talking to him, Khloe. Being civil long enough for him to tell you what you've wanted to know for all these years."

"You mean why he left and never called once?"

"Yes."

"Mom, I don't have time for this," I said a bit more harshly than I needed to.

I sighed, seeing the hurt on my mother's face. "Sorry. I'm sorry. It's just—literally everyone who has come into this library today has asked me the same question. Have I seen Jasper? Have I spoken to him? Do I know anything about him? Has he come by? I'm over it. I'm done with this day. Yay, he's back. Woo hoo. Now, we can go on about our lives just like we did when he first left us all in the dust?"

"He lost his parents, Khloe, and moved away from everyone he knew. I know you remember how devastating that was."

"Yeah, we all do. That still didn't give him the right to break my heart like that."

Mom pursed her lips, and I knew I had talked myself into a corner.

"Shit," I hissed.

"Language. Talk to him, Khloe. Be reasonable long enough to get the closure you need. No one's trying to matchmake you. Unless that's what you want."

"No, that's not even remotely what I want."

She nodded. "Fine, then. But be nice when you—"

"Khlo?"

I froze. My heart stopped in my chest, and my knees stiffened. I slowly peered over my mother's shoulder, knowing damn good and well who would be standing there.

His bright emerald eyes shone at me.

"Hey, Khlo," Jasper said quietly.

"Uh, she doesn't like to be called that," Matt interjected with some primitive need to protect me in some way.

Mom rubbed my back and whispered in my ear. "Be. Nice."

Then she left, brushing by Jasper, patting his back, and smiling at him. As if he were part of the family again.

A family he abandoned.

My stare ran down his body as the two of them stood

there. Kent and Jasper. And Mom was right. He did look good. He was much taller than I remembered; he had towered over me by at least a foot. His hair was disheveled in that sexy, stylish way, and he had stubble on his jawline, like a grown man. And his muscles—holy hell, the man had them pulled taut all over his body. His tanned skin glistened in the fluorescent library lights, and a hint of a tattoo peeked from under the collar of his shirt.

"What do you want, Kent?" I asked.

My eyes flickered over to him, and I tried ignoring Jasper. I heard the irritation in my voice. I saw Kent wince at it, even.

"I'll be outside," Kent said by way of an answer.

When he left, Jasper didn't follow.

I cleared my throat as my eyes returned back to his. Those bright emerald eyes glistened as a smile crossed his face. It was soft. Miniscule, really. But it reached his eyes. They crinkled softly, and I tried my best to quell the traitorous flutter in my chest.

"So I guess the rumors are true," I said.

He nodded. "Yep."

His voice had changed, too. It was deeper and a little more gravelly.

And damn did it sound good to my ears. *Get a grip, Khloe. He broke your heart, remember?*

"So, not a fan of the nickname anymore?" Jasper asked.

"No," I said plainly.

He nodded softly before the doors of the library opened again, followed by a bark.

"What the—?"

"No, no, no. Piper. Wait in the car," Jasper said.

"No dogs are allowed in—ah!"

The golden retriever made his way for me and jumped up to my shoulders. The dog's paws landed against my chest, and he started licking my neck. I backed away from the dog. But with every step I took, the dog moved with me like we were dancing.

"Please get down."

"Piper. Bad girl. Down. Right now."

A sharp whistle came out of nowhere, and I stumbled back. The dog pushed off me and fell to the floor, but it didn't stop barking. I plugged my ears as Matthew rushed from around the front desk and shooed the dog out the door. But Jasper didn't follow. My fingers fell from my ears, and I glared at him, dusting myself off as he reached for me. But when I shot him another look, his hand quickly fell back to his side.

"That's Piper. She's a police dog. And a support animal, and my best friend," Jasper said.

I laughed bitterly. "So, my place went to a dog."

His face sank, and I didn't care.

"Look, Khlo—"

"Khloe," I said hotly.

"Khloe, I know you're busy. I just wanted to come by and say hi. Kent is giving me a ride around the town. Getting me used to the new areas."

"Had you come back once in a while, there wouldn't have been a need for that."

He nodded slowly. "I know. Trust me, I—"

"Trust you?"

"Oh, boy," Matt murmured.

"Trust you?" I asked again.

Jasper held his hands up in a defensive gesture. "I just came by to see you. That's all."

"To see me."

"Yeah. I saw your mom at lunch. I saw Quinn this morning."

I took another step forward. "And you just thought you'd

finish off the whole family? Get those boxes checked off your list so you can feel better?"

He flinched at my hard tone. "It's not like that."

"You know what, Jasper? It's fine. I don't really care. I need to get back to work."

"Khlo, please—"

"Khloe," I said sharply, my voice rising.

He sighed. "I'm sorry. I shouldn't have come."

"No, you shouldn't have. You can see yourself out the same way you came in."

CHAPTER 6

JASPER

"You get what you wanted outta that?"

I sighed. "Yeah. I'm good. Just drive."

Piper barked and panted in the back seat of the cruiser as Kent pulled around the rotunda of the library. As my gaze fell out the window, my mind swirled. I hadn't expected things to go over well with Khloe at all, but I didn't expect things to get that heated.

She was very angry with me.

And rightfully so, asshole.

I wanted to see her, yes, but on my terms or hers, not an ambush. After going into town for some food and running into her mother, it was almost too coincidental that I'd come across Kent eating in his car outside. He offered me a ride home, and suddenly, we were headed for the library.

"Why did you bring me here again?" I asked.

I looked over at him as we pulled onto the main road.

"All I did was offer. You took me up on it," he said.

"I'm pretty sure you offered me a ride home, and then we ended up at the library."

"After I asked you if you wanted to go over there and see her. You could've said no."

"You made it seem as if she wasn't upset with me."

He snickered. "How the hell did I do that? I asked if you wanted to see her, you said 'is that a good idea?' and I said—"

"'I guess there have been worse ideas. How angry can she really be?'"

"Yeah. And I guess we know how angry she can really be now."

I shook my head. "Great."

"Hey, look. Khloe and I have been tight ever since she got married. I was her husband's best friend, and when he died—"

"Khloe got married?" I interrupted, feeling like I'd been gut-punched.

Kent sighed. "Yeah, man. She got married. I was the best man at their wedding. And when John died, she was wrecked. Her family was there for her, sure. But so was I. Because her other best friend disappeared on her and never came back."

I nodded slowly. "How did he die?"

"Heart attack. Dropped dead on the street in the middle of his morning run."

I shook my head. "Shit."

"And I figured that if she was going to implode on you— or explode, for that matter—it'd be better for me to be there for both of your sakes instead of it happening in private."

"For my protection or hers?"

"Mainly for her. I know she needs closure. I know all about what happened between you two. How you left. How you never called. How she tried to track you down after she graduated."

I blinked. "Wait, what?"

He nodded. "Yeah. I know all about that shit. According

to her, she tried tracking you down in Vegas after she graduated. Convinced her family to take a two-week vacation there and did her best to try and figure it out. To find you. Until she realized how big Las Vegas really is. You know, city limits versus Strip limits and all that."

"She tried to come find me?"

"Yep. She never once gave up, until after that trip."

I felt sick to my stomach. "I guess you being there for her during that encounter was the best move, yeah."

"I know it was. You've been gone for a long time. And look, it's great you're back and all, but don't expect a red carpet or anything."

"Trust me, I didn't. Just, next time? Let's make a plan before we go charging into something like that."

He nodded. "Oh, and if Khloe decides to kill you, I will help her hide the body. Just saying."

Just then, the police radio in the car came to life, and I felt myself jumping into action, despite the fact that it wasn't my first day yet.

"All units within a radius of 302 Broadstone Road, be advised. Subject is an underaged white male. Elderly man says the kid's trying to break into his garage. Unit response times, go."

Kent reached for the radio. "This is cruiser 1801, I'm 10-8 in the area. ETA, less than two minutes."

"Copy that, 1801. Everyone else, 10-100."

"Why do I recognize that address?" I asked.

"Eh, it's Old Man Hauston's home. I swear he's got more kids breaking into his place than anyone I've ever met."

"Mr. Hauston? The science teacher?"

"I think he retired a couple of years ago. But, yeah. I think he taught science."

I nodded. "Yeah. That's my old science teacher from high school."

"Well, we're about to go figure out why some punk kid is breaking into his garage."

Kent turned on the sirens and whipped a U-turn in the middle of the road. I hung on, clinging to the door as Piper went into position, with her nose down, her eyes forward, and her body focused. It was amazing to me how she could quickly go into work mode like that. Be on alert. Be at my side. Attentive to my needs as well as the needs of the field.

When we pulled into Mr. Hauston's driveway, I heard his voice.

"Get the hell off my property, you little asshole!"

"Give me my bike back!" the kid yelled.

"Not if I have anything to do with it. Are you with that gang of googly-eyed kids? Huh? Pipe cleaners with eyes that keep egging my house?"

"Officer! Officer! This man has my bike!"

A blinding flash took over my vision. I felt the cold of Piper's nose against my neck as she nuzzled it up and down, up and down, trying to regulate my erratic heart-beat. The yelling ripped me back, flashes of my men yelling in the field bombarding my vision. I reached for the door and felt Piper's paw settle against the top of my hand, stopping me as her nose continued to massage my carotid.

Up and down.

Up and down.

Up and down.

"Good girl," I whispered.

I felt myself teetering on the edge of an attack. Another image flashed to the forefront of my mind. An explosion, the sound echoing off the corners of my mind, followed by soldiers scrambling. Someone yelling for a medic.

"Medic! I need a medic!"

"Medic! Someone get me a fucking medic!"

"Officer! My mom's going to kill me if I don't get my bike back!"

The world quickly came back into focus, and I drew in a deep breath. I reached back and scratched behind Piper's ears, letting her know I was okay. I thought it best not to get out of the car, especially since I wasn't in my official uniform, or clocked in for that matter. I was worried, though. Worried that my PTSD might get the best of me in the field. But as I watched Kent work, I took in what he did— how he handled Mr. Hauston, how he disarmed the kid without once reaching for his weapon.

Such different territory from Vegas.

Kent looked back at me with concern on his face. His stare flitted around, and then he nodded in my general direction. Shit. Did he know what just happened? I'd get fired before I ever got into the office tomorrow. I sat back and heaved a heavy sigh. Piper rested her snout against my shoulder from beyond the seat in the cruiser. As I drew in deep breaths, I watched Kent shoo the kid away on his bike before wrapping things up with Mr. Hauston.

He dropped down into the car before backing out of the driveway.

"Apparently, Hauston has had his bike for a couple of days," Kent said.

"Really?" I asked.

"Yep. Kid was trying to get in there because Hauston had his bike. Guess Hauston's deciding to steal from the kids in order to teach them a lesson in stealing from him. I let him off with a warning. This time."

I nodded.

"And before you ask? Don't worry. We'll help you work around it."

I paused. "What?"

He shrugged. "The PTSD. You aren't the only one here on

the Canaan Force that deals with it. We'll help you work around it like we do the other guys. All right?"

I nodded slowly. "Good to know."

"Want me to take you home?"

"Sure. Yeah. I should get unpacked and get some rest for tomorrow anyway."

"Yep. Due at eight in the morning, sharp. Chief doesn't like it when we're late. So, don't be."

"I'm never late."

"That's what they all say."

Kent chuckled as I directed him on how to get to my place. While I enjoyed the ride around, it felt odd hanging out with him. Hanging out with Khloe's dead husband's best friend. Hanging out with the guy who'd apparently taken my place. Not that I was pissed about it or anything—Khloe deserved a loyal friend. She deserved everything, really. The world on a silver platter.

Not that I'd be the one to give it to her.

She looked outstanding.

Even as I stood in my driveway, waving Kent off, I couldn't get her off my mind. The last time I'd seen Khloe in glasses, she had been in middle school. And oh, how wonderful they looked on her. Those brown eyes—though mad—still sparkled with those flecks of green. Flecks of color that reminded me of Christmas and the trees we went hunting for and decorated together. The smell of pine would always fill our nostrils from room to room, no matter where we went.

"You really stepped in it, didn't you?" I murmured to myself.

I scratched behind Piper's ear before we headed into the house. It had been a whirlwind of a day being back, and I needed some rest. I closed the front door behind me and locked it. Piper jumped up, nudging the lights on as she made her way around the house. I grinned as the lights flicked on, illuminating my childhood home.

House, really. It didn't much feel like a home.

I walked into the kitchen and stood in the middle of it. Everywhere I looked, there was dust. I opened the cabinets, and the plates were coated in it. I picked up a mug, and they were filled with it. I walked over to the fridge and opened it up, staring at the bare expanse.

Nothing in it.

Kind of like my soul.

"What do you think about pizza for dinner?" I asked.

Piper barked as she came rushing into the kitchen.

"Yeah, yeah. I gotta get your food out of the bed of the truck. You hungry, girl? Yes, you are. I bet you are, sweet girl."

I dipped down and let her lick my face. I scratched behind her ears and patted down her back. I sat on my ass and let her run me over, my back falling to the kitchen floor. The dust was almost too much. I'd have to clean this place up or have it professionally cleaned. One or the other. Then again, I didn't sleep much most nights. If it wasn't insomnia, it was nightmares waking me up every hour.

I had enough time to clean it myself if I wanted to.

"All right," I grunted as I stood up, "first, we get you some food. Then, we get me some food. Then, we clean. How's that sound?"

Piper barked before she started whimpering.

"I know, I know. You don't like vacuums. But really. Have you seen this place?"

She sighed and flopped down at my feet, which made me chuckle.

"You can't keep me here all night, Pipes. This house needs a good clean-down. No matter how you feel about it."

She yawned before grumbling at me, and I reached down to pet her head.

"I promise I won't run the vacuum for long. Just enough to make this place smell a little less musty."

Then, I made my way for the front door, ready to unpack the bed of my truck, get Piper some food, and then order myself a nice pizza. Maybe that place on the corner of Main and Lexington was still open.

Because damn it, they had the best selection of toppings out of anywhere in Canaan.

CHAPTER 7

KHLOE

I dreaded every day I came into work now. Every morning, when I turned on the light, I wondered if Jasper would be there waiting for me, staring at me and wanting to talk. Every time I walked out of the library for the day, I wondered if he would be standing by my car. He'd been in town an entire week; surely, he had access to the precinct and their files by now. He could track down anything about me. The kind of car I drove now. Where I lived. Hell, he could probably use some sort of software to track where I was via my phone every second of every day.

This is Jay we're talking about. Not some psychopathic stalker.

No. Jasper.

Jay left a long time ago.

The woman before me, who was the head librarian before she appointed me, had been there for me as a child and watched me grow up. I used to cut through her backyard with Jasper and pick dead weeds out of her yard to blow the seeds around. Miss Honeycutt never married. There were rumors that she'd had several trysts. The talk of the town, Mom always called her. But she always had a smile on her face, and she always sat in that office, right behind the door that held my name on it, manning her station until the day she passed away.

Finding that note of hers that named me head librarian had been an incredible moment. Incredibly sobering, too. She'd hired me when I chose to stay in town for college instead of going away to be the big, bad computer science nerd and then supported me when I dropped out of community college to work at the library full-time.

Mom hadn't been happy about that. Not one bit. But, school didn't hold the same flair for me during my senior year. I wasn't excited about it. I didn't want to sit mindlessly in classes and listen to older people drone on about stupid shit. I wanted to be working, paving my own way.

Preferably, while not around people.

"Good afternoon, Khloe!"

I jumped at Matt's voice. "Hey there. Hey. How—what are you doing here?"

He paused. "I work the afternoon shift today. Did you forget?"

"No, no. No. I didn't...forget, necessarily."

He grinned. "Just slipped your mind?"

I snapped. "There we go. Slipped my mind."

"So, I take it tonight's event slipped your mind, too?"

I blinked. "What?"

He chuckled. "The First Friday event?"

Oh shit. "With the police department."

"That's the one. I'm here to help close before we set it up."

"Great."

"Don't sound too enthusiastic now. I figured you'd miss me."

"No, no. It's not that."

He leaned against the front desk. "Want to talk about it?"

"Not particularly. Why don't you clock in, and we'll get

started setting up." Miss Honeycutt had started the tradition. It had been going on for as long as I could remember. Every first Friday of the month from 5:30 to 9:00, there were drink and food vendors, farmers came out to sell their fresh goods, and we got to advertise the library's services and drum up donations, and generally remind the community that we were still there.

And the police department sent a couple officers to do community outreach.

Fuck.

I knew that I would need to get used to the idea that Jasper was back in town and that I'd run into him from time to time. I needed to figure out a way to be okay with that. But I simply wasn't ready just yet.

The day flew by quicker than I wanted it to, and by the time the library closed down for the event, it felt like doomsday was upon me. We rushed around to help get the vendors set up. Matt cleared his throat and gargled with salt-water like he was about to give some spectacular performance. I unlocked the doors to the first level of the library we set up specifically for the kids, with craft tables to reading corners to shelves of books they could check out with me while I answered their questions and stood behind the front desk.

Maybe Jasper won't be here tonight.

That was the best-case scenario. Worst case, however, I used his dog as an excuse for him to not come near me in the library.

"Khloe?"

"Yeah, Matt?"

"Kent is here."

The tone of his voice told me everything I needed to know. Jasper was here, too. And so was that dog. But without its paws on my shoulders and its tongue slathering my face, I took a moment to get a good look at the animal and had to admit to myself that it was quite beautiful. And attentive.

She stayed right up against Jasper's side, her head underneath his palm.

Huh.

"Looks like a trauma dog. Or one of those support animals," Matt said.

I nodded slowly, remembering how he'd described her. "I think that's what he said, yeah."

"I wonder what for."

I shrugged. "Probably something from the military."

"Maybe he's got PTSD."

"Or maybe it's one of those dogs that can sense a drop in insulin. Maybe he's got diabetes."

"Don't sound so hopeful," Matt snickered.

I saw Kent walking for the doors, and I drew in a deep breath. I'd made it through losing Jasper, burying my husband, and moving on with my life—I could deal with this. I was strong enough to do that. Kent came over and hugged me, very tight and very long, just how I loved his hugs.

"I'm sorry," he murmured.

I sighed. "Warn me next time, yeah?"

"I just figured it was easier to just get it over with."

"Not your call, and you know that."

"Had to protect the new guy from getting killed and all that."

I snickered. "Asshole."

He grinned. "That's Officer Asshole to you."

I giggled as his hands fell against my shoulders. He held me out away from him and smiled down at me with that cheeky little smile of his. He brought me back in for one last hug, and I sighed heavily, releasing all of my tension against his body. Kent's hugs were the best. He had been there for me during a time where I'd pushed everyone else away, where I'd built up walls with cement and rebar to keep the pain and the hurt at bay.

And he came slamming through it like a wrecking ball without any shits given to the world.

"Love you, Khloe."

I nodded. "Love you, too, Kent."

He squeezed my shoulders. "Ready for the event?"

I sighed. "Ready as I'll ever be."

I peered around his body and saw Jasper heading for the library doors, then stopping. Heading for the doors, then stopping. Like he was constantly talking himself out of the idea.

"Just let him bring the damn dog in so he can see you. He's been shaking like a leaf in the wind all day," Kent said.

I rolled my eyes. "Fine. But please don't let that dog jump on me again."

"Piper won't jump you when she's working."

"And what exactly does the dog do?"

"Well, for starters, she alerts us to any panic attacks Jasper might have."

I cleared my throat, trying to push away the brief feeling of sympathy that flipped in my gut.

"Okay. If the dog doesn't jump on me like last time, we're all good," I said.

"Thanks. You're the best," Kent said.

He beckoned for Jasper, and the man practically leaped through the doors. Piper stayed next to him, never once inching more than he did. Jasper stopped in front of me and reached out a hand. Begrudgingly, I took it.

"This looks great in here," he said as he shook my hand.

I pulled my hand away quickly as electricity shot up my arm. Damn it. His touch still had the same effect on me that it had always had. And I hated it.

"Thanks," I said, hardly able to keep the waver out of my voice.

I silently admonished my body for its betrayal when Jasper was near. He'd left, he'd forgotten about me, he'd broken my heart. There was no reason I should still get all warm and tingly in his presence.

"Hey, I'm Matt. I'm the children's librarian here."

Matt's hand came out of nowhere, and he shook Jasper's.

"Nice to meet you," Jasper said.

His deep voice made my stomach jump and my heart slam against my ribcage.

Pull it together, Khloe.

"So, you ready for the first Friday event?" Jasper asked.

"And that's my cue. The kids are waiting. Khloe, want to introduce me?" Matt asked.

I looked over at him and saw him nodding in the direction of the story-time mat. And sure enough, there were throngs of children sitting, waiting as patiently as kids could.

"Thanks for coming," I said to Jasper. Our eyes connected, and I felt my heart stop in my chest. His eyes hadn't changed one bit. His face had worn with age, and the stubble on his jawline had been shaved clean. His hair was parted cleanly to one side, though still pretty long. But his eyes—those beautiful eyes I had fallen in love with as a teenage girl—still looked just like they had in my dreams.

"I have to get going," I said softly.

Jasper nodded, then held out his arm. And together, the four of us made our way to the story-time mat. The kids clapped and cheered before I put my finger to my lips, silencing their applause. I stood in front of Matt's chair and locked my hands together, making sure to count each and every head.

For this first story, we had thirty-one kids, up from the twenty-two we had during last month's event.

"All right, kiddos. If you're new to our event, welcome," I said.

The kids smiled at me, and I felt Jasper's stare against my face.

"Our story tonight is *Lyle, Lyle Crocodile*, and it's my favorite story. I grew up with it as a kid," I said.

"She really did," Jasper said.

My eyes whipped over to his, and the kids turned their heads.

"I mean, it was her favorite book. I remember her reading it all the time. Well into middle school," he said.

The kids giggled, and our gazes locked. And as he held my stare, it looked as if he was trying to apologize without using words.

"Officer Willem is right. Back when I was a little girl, I used to read this book under my covers all the time. And now, our very own Mr. Matthew is going to read it for you guys tonight. How does that sound?" I asked.

"Yeah!" the kids exclaimed.

I put my finger to my lips. "If you're really quiet, he might come out. Are you ready? Can you be very, very quiet?"

The more they settled down, the closer Matt crept with the book.

"Oh, kids. I think I see him," I whispered.

They gasped before one of the kids let out a loud "shh!"

"Very quiet," I whispered.

"Hello, kids!" Matt exclaimed.

He jumped out of the corner, and the kids jumped. Everyone fell apart in laughter, and Jasper's boisterous sound filled the room. My eyes snapped straight to his, and I caught that broad smile again, the one that crinkled his eyes and ignited a fire behind that stare of his. I stepped off to the side and let Matt take the reins. But Jasper's eyes followed me, and he suddenly appeared at my side.

"You were great up there," he murmured.

I peeked up at him. "Thanks."

"You were always good with kids, you know."

I nodded softly. "I guess."

"I'm sorry for your loss, Khlo."

His words hit me hard, and I felt my eyes watering.

"Please don't call me that," I whispered, my voice hitching.

"I'm sorry for everything."

The gravelly sound of his voice made my heart surge with life. I was a widow. At one point in time, a dedicated wife. I didn't need to be feeling this way about some boy that left all those years ago. But every time he stole a glance my way, electricity sizzled down my spine. Every time he murmured something to me, I felt my knees weaken. The heat of his body called to me. The smell of his aftershave filled my nostrils, causing my heart to skip a beat. I was caught between my past and my future, struggling to make sense of why Jasper still had this effect on me; why he still made me feel this way after all these years.

You're in hot water, Khloe.

Yet, part of me didn't seem to care as I scooted ever so closer to his body.

CHAPTER 8

JASPER

With my first day of work behind me, I felt more prepared to tackle the real problem: unpacking my shit. With Piper circling my legs, I picked up my small box of books. I nudged my mother's library open with my hip and drew in the smell of, well, dust. Not as much, though. I just needed to throw a window open, and things would be fine. I set the box of books down, my hands already sweating.

I hadn't been inside these rooms for so long.

I looked over toward my mother's chair and saw her sitting there. She had her leg curled up against her chest, with her heel digging into the cushion, her arm wrapped around the outside of her leg while she held her book in both of her hands. She always had the oddest ways of curling up while reading. And as her hair fell into her face, I smiled.

While my heart tore itself apart.

"Mom," I murmured.

She looked up at me and smiled. Those dazzling green eyes, ones I'd inherited from her. She smiled, and my heart came to life. Then, she faded away, leaving nothing but the imprint of her body against the chair and a small dip in the cushion where she always sat her heel.

I walked over and slid my fingers across it.

"Oh, Mom," I whispered.

Unpacking was a nightmare. My palms sweated as I scooted her books over, disturbing them for the first time in twelve years. I put my books on the shelves next to hers. I didn't have many of them. But, each one of them I'd bought with her in mind. I read them, even though I hated reading. I read them to remind me of her and her love for reading. Every year, I promised to get through two books, just for her, one that got me to her birthday in the middle of July, and one that got me to her favorite time of year.

Christmas.

I sighed as I scooped up the cardboard box. I walked over to the banister and tossed it over the edge. It fell to the floor, smacking against the hardwood. Then, I reached for yet another box.

One that belonged in my father's cigar room.

I wasn't a smoker. But every year on his birthday, I had one just for him. I was running out, too. The cigars I'd stolen from his collection twelve years ago were almost gone. I had two left. One for his birthday in a couple of months, and one for next year. After that, I'd have to figure out where to buy them or find a new tradition.

No. I'd have to figure out where to buy them.

I licked my lips and paused. I closed my eyes and stood at the entryway to that damn room. After all these years, I still smelled traces of tobacco in the door, wafting underneath the crack of it. My hands shook. The small box I held wavered as I started blinking rapidly. My eyes burned. My heart clenched. I drew in a broken breath before I reached my foot out, softly pushing the door open.

How the room still looked hazy, I wasn't sure.

Or maybe it was hazy because of my tears.

"You don't have to live forever. You just have to live."

I shook my head as I walked into the room. My father's voice echoed off the corners of my mind as snippets of that damn book rushed to the forefront. *Tuck Everlasting.* I still didn't know why my father enjoyed that book as much as he did. But every time I sat down at this closed door, he picked it up and read it to me, always picking up from where he left off the last time.

"Life's got to be lived, no matter how long or short. You got to take what comes."

I sniffled deeply as I set the small box down on his chair. The gaudy bronze-and-red chair was high-backed and shining. Still, after all these years. I started pulling out the few things I had in the box. The golden lighter. The new butane fluid I had purchased. The two cigars left. I set them where they needed to be, in their exact places around the desk. Then, I dropped the box at my feet before turning myself around.

With my palms pointed down and my knees unlocked, I readied myself to sit. I couldn't bring myself to do it, though. A tear worked its way down my cheek as Piper whimpered from the doorway. Fucking hell, this was harder than I ever imagined it to be. I slid my hands quickly into the pockets of my pants, another tear leaking down my face.

"Don't be afraid of death. Be afraid of the unlived life."

It was like Dad's memory was torturing me at this point.

My feet carried me quickly out of the room. I rushed back downstairs and finished unpacking the few things I had brought with me. The amount was meager, though. Five boxes and two duffel bags that contained the whole of my life. Then again, that's what happened when you spent most of my past several years abroad. In the barracks. In a bunk bed. Or living out of a seven-hundred-square-foot apartment over a bakery in the middle of Vegas.

I stood in the middle of the downstairs hallway and slowly turned around. It was as if that damn storage shed was whispering to me. Calling to me. Haunting me in my nightmares. I stared down through the kitchen and out the window, taking in the small white dot in the backyard. A massive shed that, when cleared out, wasn't much smaller than my apartment back in Vegas.

But it wasn't cleared out.

"Shit," I whispered.

When my aunt cleaned out most of the house, she put my parents' things in there. Their clothes. My mother's jewelry. Things that were precious to them that she didn't know what to do with. With the keys to the house came the keys to that damn shed, and I didn't know if I was ready to pilfer through and investigate it.

Maybe I can just leave it.

"In, and out."

My therapist's voice sounded so heavily in my ears that I jumped.

"In, and out."

"All right, all right," I murmured.

I closed my eyes and drew in a deep breath. I felt my stomach expanding. I felt my toes curling into the ground to root me. I cracked my neck and forced my shoulders to release, concentrating on relaxing my body. Unlocking my jaw. Unfurrowing my brow.

"In, and out."

The more breaths I took, the more relaxed I felt. My therapist back in Vegas used to walk me through the exercises. She taught me how to become more in tune with my body and with the tension I carried.

"In, and out," I whispered.

Piper nudged my hand, and my eyes fluttered open. And when my gaze fell onto that white dot, I locked back up again. My knees stiffened. My jaw clenched. My brow furrowed and my back straightened. Nope. Not today. Maybe another day.

Or maybe never.

"Come on, Pipes. Let's go get some food."

Piper barked with approval, and we headed for my truck. I whistled at her, motioning for her to get in the bed of the truck. On sunny days like this one, I let her ride back there to get some fresh air and feel the sun on her back. But just as I went to open my door to climb in, I paused.

Because I saw Khloe getting out of her car up the road.

I stood there, watching how she fiddled with her phone, how she tucked her purse underneath her arm. She pushed her glasses up the bridge of her nose, and I smiled. I hadn't seen that motion in a very long time. Glasses suited her, though. They always had. I had to admit, part of my heart broke the day she decided to wear contacts regularly instead of wearing her glasses.

"Stay here, girl," I said as I made my way toward Khloe.

I didn't know what the hell I'd say once I got to her, but Friday had been fantastic. Her hand in mine had felt amazing. And having her stand beside me during that story time felt incredible. And I could have sworn she kept stepping closer to me.

That, alone, was enough to give me hope.

"Jasper?"

I waved as I stood at the bottom of the driveway.

"Hey there, Khlo—eeee."

She laughed despite herself. "How are you?"

"Uh, I'm good. Good. Yeah, Piper and I are just going to get some food somewhere. Just got done unpacking my things."

She nodded. "That's good."

"I just—saw you standing over here. Figured I'd come say hi."

"Well, hi." Her answers were brief, concise, unemotional.

Okay, maybe not a good idea. "Well, nice seeing you again."

"You, too."

Fuck. "Say hi to Quinn and your parents for m—"

"Why did you really come over here?"

I blinked. "What?"

"Why did you really come over here, Jasper?"

"I—I just—"

She looked at me with that prying stare. Khloe always did know how to read me. How to stare right through the bullshit and drill down to the truth. So, why continue to hide it from her?

"Piper and I are going to get lunch in order to avoid unpacking the shed out back. It's, you know, filled with some stuff I'm not ready for yet," I said.

Her face softened. "Some comfort food before the hard stuff. I get that."

I nodded slowly. "Pretty pathetic, huh?"

"Not at all. Especially after what you went through."

"Guess I'm just procrastinating. You know, delaying what has to happen eventually."

"No one can blame you for that."

We stared at one another for a moment before I drew in a deep breath.

"Well, I'll see you around," I said.

"Whenever you come back, if you need help, let me know. Okay?"

Her words shocked me. "Help?"

Khloe nodded. "Yeah. You know, going through that shed. I'm assuming it's got your parent's things in it. I remember seeing your aunt here a time or two."

"Yeah. She was."

"Let me know if you need any help with it at all."

"That—actually sounds really nice. I'm going to take you up on that offer."

"What time do you think you'd be back from lunch?" she asked.

I shook my head. "I don't know. I'm not hungry, but I guess food's the only thing that came to mind to get me away from the house."

Her gaze held mine before she sighed.

"My parents can wait. I was just popping by to say hey, anyway. Come on. Let's go get started. Work you up a good appetite," she said.

She started walking toward me as my eyes widened. She brushed past me, and the scent of her perfume dragged me along with her. I watched her hair billow back. Her shirt flowed wondrously over her soft curves. And as her jeans clung to her legs, I tried my best not to stare at the swaying of her hips.

Though the movement was mesmerizing.

"Piper, come!" I commanded.

I gave a piercing whistle, and she hopped out of the truck. I snapped and pointed next to me, watching as she went alert. Her snout pointed down, and her tail curled against her. As she walked with me, I felt her fur against my down-facing palm, preparing me for something I already felt coming.

The closer we got to the shed, the more my heart hammered. I stopped to catch my breath and felt Khloe staring at me. Waiting for me. I didn't want her to see me like this. I wanted to tell her I'd catch her some other time with this bullshit. But she guided me forward with a kind smile and that damn perfume of hers.

"All right. You got the keys?" she asked as we reached the shed.

My trembling hand slid into my pocket, and I pulled out the set. I handed them to Khloe, and she quirked an eyebrow before taking them from me. Sweat soaked through the back of my shirt, and I felt my heart surging to life. As Piper started whining, I watched Khloe open the shed door.

And the smell alone sent me to the ground.

I drew in shuddering breaths as my chest felt as if it were caving in. Piper jumped up and immediately began massaging the vein against my neck I felt bulging. So, I gripped her coat of fur. The world around me tilted, and it grew harder to breathe. My toes curled, trying to root myself to a ground that wasn't there because I was sitting flat on my ass in the grass of my backyard.

Unable to move.

"Jasper, can you hear me? It's okay. You're safe. Jasper, can you hear me? It's okay. You're safe."

Piper continued massaging, and my eyes fluttered closed. I gripped my dog tighter, and I focused on Khloe's voice. A kind voice, coaching me through my panic. I drank it all in. Memories of my parents bombarded my mind. I felt myself spiraling, making me sick to my stomach. I squeezed my eyes shut. I did my best to rein in my fears. And as my chest finally unlocked itself, I drew in a deep breath through my nose, trying not to gasp so hard for air.

As the world came back into focus, Piper stopped massaging my neck. My hand loosened against her fur, and I felt something warm against my knee. Against my chest. Against my cheek. My eyes fell open, and I looked down, watching as Khloe's hands came into view. I blinked back the tears as beads of sweat dripped down my face, falling to her skin.

"It's okay. I'm right here," Khloe murmured gently.

Her hands rubbed circles against my knee and my heart. It thudded painfully against my chest. But my blood pressure didn't skyrocket. I felt myself settling down. The gasping stopped. My legs relaxed. My heart settled down, and the world stopped tilting, which cleared up the sickness in my stomach.

"Do you need me to get you inside?" Khloe asked.

I shook my head. "One. Two. Three. Four."

She whispered the numbers with me as I worked on the breathing exercises. As I counted down, I slowly rooting myself back into reality.

Khloe continued drawing soft circles. "Ten. Nine. Eight. Seven."

With one final breath, I cleared my throat. I eased myself off the ground and felt her grip me as she helped me up. She tried to steady me as I teetered, and my cheeks flushed with embarrassment. But more than that, I was shocked at how easy it had been for her to help me. It felt good, having her there. It felt comfortable, feeling her touch. It felt wonderful, hearing her voice in my ear.

God, I've missed you. "I have to do this," I croaked.

Khloe started rubbing my back as my gaze found hers.

"I have to do this because if I don't, this shed will just haunt me until I do. Which won't do me any favors."

She nodded. "Well, whenever you're ready, I'm right here with you. Okay?"

And with her words, my heart skipped a beat.

CHAPTER 9

KHLOE

Panic attack. I had just witnessed Jasper have a major panic attack. And it took all the energy I had to keep my own panic at bay just to help him. I mean, I didn't know if I had helped. For all I knew, I'd made things worse, and he simply couldn't tell me that. Or didn't want to. I guess my heart was always meant to break for him. Because as I stood there, rubbing his back, I felt the tattered remnants of whatever was left of it shatter for him again. In those moments where he couldn't catch his breath, I didn't see a grown man. I didn't see a grizzled vet. I saw the scared teenager from the emergency room. The one who could barely talk through his tears. The one who'd collapsed against me when the nurse told him his parents had died.

The one who'd comforted me on his departure instead of the other way around.

I hope I was able to help you this time.

Jasper turned toward the opened door of the shed, and my hand fell away from him. He walked in front of me, with his dog clinging tight against his side. I watched the darkness of that shed outline his frame, threatening to eat him alive as he stood there.

He still looked like that high school boy whose world had been turned upside down.

Go easy on him. He's struggling, just like you.

I drew in a deep breath and walked up beside him. I slipped my hand into his and held it. Tightly. I looked up at him and found his stare, still laced with a few tears. And as I reached up, I wiped the sweat from his brow.

"Whenever you're ready, the light's on my side," I said.

"I'll never be ready, Khlo. But I have to do this."

I reached for the light and flipped the switch, illuminating the space around us. As dust flew around in the air, I felt Jasper squeeze the life out of my hand. We walked into the shed together, barely able to move with all the stuff in there, but it was all neatly laid out, all of the boxes labeled and organized. The racks of clothes were situated in every corner of the shed, giving off an old scent even I remembered from my childhood.

The rose notes of his mother's perfume and the tobacco from his father.

"Oh, God," I whispered.

I had to be strong for him. I had to make sure Jasper didn't feel a need to comfort me during a time like this. But staring at all this stuff hurt my heart. I blinked back the burning sensation behind my eyes and squeezed Jasper's hand. I pressed closer against him, seeking the comfort of his warmth.

"What do I do with the clothes?" he asked.

I thought about his question. "I suppose that depends. Do you want your father's clothes?"

"I don't know."

"Then maybe going through them and picking out what you don't want is a place to start. If you wouldn't wear those clothes anyway, you can donate them. Same with your mother. And the clothes you think you might wear, you can keep."

He nodded.

"But we can do those later. Right now, we've got boxes in front of us to look through."

He sighed. "Yeah, we do."

"The first one I saw was labeled 'bone china.'"

"Probably my parents' wedding china they received."

I nodded slowly. "Do you want to keep that?"

He shook his head. "I—I don't know, Khlo. Khloe. Sorry."

"It's okay. You're fine."

I panned my gaze ahead and slowly guided him deeper into the shed. We walked around the boxes, reading out their labels, and tried to figure out whether Jasper needed those things or not. It was a hard task. He didn't know about a lot of the stuff. But there were some things that were a hard pass.

"I don't think you need your father's underwear," I said.

"Nope. Definitely not."

"Or your mother's—"

"Don't say it. Just, no."

I giggled. "Good enough for me."

"Or her shoes."

"Your mother had such fabulous shoes."

"You can pick some out if you'd like."

I paused. "I don't know. Maybe."

He squeezed my hand. "Offer's there if you want it. Same goes with her jewelry and her purses."

I drew in a sharp breath. "Why don't we try to figure out what you want to take back into the house now? That might be easier. What do you not have in the house right now?"

"Uh, well. I don't have extra linens for my bed."

"All right. What else?"

"Only got a couple of towels."

"Good, good. Making a list. Great."

"If there are pots and pans in here, that would be nice, too."

I pointed. "I think that box says, 'pots and pans.'"

We navigated over to the box, picking things up and putting them down elsewhere. After digging through part of the shed, we had what we needed: two extra boxes of linens for all the beds in the house, three boxes of pots and pans, Christmas decorations for the impending holiday season, and two boxes full of towels and other odd bathroom items.

I helped him haul them into the house.

"How's that stomach of yours doing?" I asked.

He sat the pots and pans onto the kitchen table and sighed.

"Hungry, actually."

"Well, there's this cute little café in town that opened up a couple years back. They have outdoor seating so, I don't think taking your dog with us would be an issue."

"Piper."

I nodded. "Right. Piper."

"You want to go to lunch with me?"

He seemed as shocked that I'd offered as I did.

"I mean, I'm pretty hungry, too. So, yeah," I said.

He stared at me for a long time. Blinking. Licking his lips. Searching my face for something.

"Thank you," Jasper said.

I simply nodded, not trusting my voice.

He whistled, and the sound made me jump. Piper came rushing into the house and jumped up to lick Jasper's face.

Noticing my expression, Jasper spoke. "Not a fan of dogs?" he asked.

"Eh, not a fan of the messes animals cause, in general."

"Huh."

I rolled my eyes. "Ready to go?"

"We can take my truck. Unless you want to follow me in your car?"

"That might be better. My parents are probably wondering why my car is in the driveway, but I'm not."

"Sorry about that."

I shook my head. "Don't be sorry. Just get in your truck and wait. Shouldn't take me too long to peel myself away from them."

I watched Piper follow Jasper out the front door and shook my head. I understood it now. Why she was so important to him. But I felt a pang of something blossom in my gut that I didn't want to own up to. How the fuck could someone be jealous of a damn dog?

Was that what I had been reduced to now?

Piper barked after me as I made my way back up the street. I jogged to my car, hoping and praying my parents didn't come out onto the porch. I figured Quinn had them busy with something anyway since she still lived at home and all. I unlocked my car and got inside, ready to lead Jasper to the cafe.

But I paused.

"Why are you having lunch with him?" I whispered to myself.

I drew in a deep breath and backed down the driveway. No use in asking questions I didn't have answers to. I drove down the road and saw Jasper's truck pull up behind me, with Piper sticking her head out the window.

Getting to the café wasn't that big of a deal. Even getting a seat outside wasn't that big of a deal. But getting Piper not to bark at every living thing that passed by was.

"Down. Piper. Cut it out," Jasper hissed.

"She do that a lot?" I asked.

"No, actually. I've never seen her this way. Piper, heel."

She whimpered and lay down, but her eyes were on everything, every person, every movement, every passer-by.

"She gonna be okay?" I asked.

Jasper scratched behind her ear. "Yeah, she should be good now."

We ordered our food but didn't talk much. Even when we got our food, things were quiet. It wasn't strained or awkward, I just didn't know what to say.

"So, you run the library now?" Jasper finally asked.

"Mm, yes. Been the head librarian for a bit now. Ever since Miss Honeycutt passed away."

"When did that happen?"

"Six or so years ago."

"You've been the head librarian for six years?"

I smiled. "Yep. That place is my domain and my solace."

"What, uh, what happened to the computer science stuff?"

I paused. "I guess things change."

His eyes searched mine. "Yeah, they do."

"So, uh, what about you? A police officer, huh? How did that come about?"

"It's really all that translated into the real world from the Marines."

"So, you were in the Marines. How long?"

"Only one tour. A bit over four years."

Don't push. Just let it come. He's a veteran, Khloe. He deserves your respect, at the very least.

The ticket for our lunch came, and he quickly swiped it up. And while I fought him on it, he refused to let me pay or split the check. It was so like Jasper, even if both of us had changed. Even as a kid, he'd never let me do things like that if I didn't have to. Taking me to get ice cream with his allowance money. Buying me coffees that we snuck underneath our parents' noses on the weekends. He'd always paid for them, insisting he foot the bill.

"Thanks for recommending this place. The food's good," Jasper said.

"I'm glad you liked it. How was your sandwich?" I asked.

"Very good. Thanksgiving, but in sandwich form. I'll have to come back and get another one soon."

He smiled at me, and that smile went straight to my gut. If I wasn't careful, I was going to lose my heart all over again.

CHAPTER 10

JASPER

My eyes popped open, and I stared up at my bedroom ceiling. Something shifted against my chest, and I jumped, feeling Piper scurry to my side. She tucked her nose against my neck, nuzzling and massaging like she had been trained to do. As the adrenaline rush wore off, I groaned.

Must've had a nightmare last night.

I didn't remember it. Thank fuck for small favors. I sighed as I inched myself up, with the sunlight barely peeking through the curtains. My feet touched down onto the cold floor, and I scrubbed my hands over my face. My stubble was growing out, reminding me that I needed to shave.

As I stood, my back twinged. I needed a new damn mattress.

"Fuck," I groaned.

A yawn escaped from my lips, unhinging my jaw. Piper jumped off the bed, already making her way downstairs. She wanted food, most likely. Time to go outside. But I wasn't ready to move yet. I wasn't ready to be awake.

What I wouldn't have done for eight nice hours of straight sleep.

These days, sleep was hard to come by. If it wasn't being interrupted by a nightmare, my body was running off a clock it had lived on for years of my life. Up before dawn. Dressed and ready for physical training. Back at my barracks and showering before the first morning formation. All of that occurring before eight in the morning. It was as if I didn't have the capability to sleep past five-thirty any longer. Six, if I was lucky. And as the morning sun continued to creep around the blackout curtains of my teenage bedroom, I forced myself to get a move on, just as Piper barked.

"I'm coming, I'm coming."

I slid my feet into my slippers. They were warm, blanketing my feet against the cold of the floor. The upstairs area always stayed cooler than the rest of the house. And damn it, I needed a better mattress. I stretched my hands over my head, feeling my entire back pop into place.

"Oh, yeah. That's the spot," I groaned.

Then, Piper barked again.

"I'm coming! Impatient thing, you."

As I shuffled down the stairs, everything from yesterday came flooding back. The panic attack in front of Khloe. The way she'd helped me through it. How embarrassed I had been afterward. And now, this apparent nightmare that forced Piper to my side last night. I thought I had been making progress back in Vegas with my therapist. But, apparently, that wasn't enough. I knew I needed to eventually find a therapist in the area. However, I figured I had a bit of time before that needed to happen.

Move that task up the list of priorities.

I let Piper out the back door before letting it hang open. I filled her bowls up with water and food, then patted down my body. Fucking hell, my cell phone was back upstairs. I groaned to myself as I started up the coffeepot. I needed to talk to someone. Anyone. Someone back in Vegas who would pick up the emergency line my therapist sent me with. With the smell of coffee filling the air, I shuffled back upstairs. I reached for my phone and sat on the edge of the bed, scrolling until I found the number.

It wasn't as if I had to scroll far, though. I only had ten contacts on my phone.

"Come on. Pick up."

I stood from the bedside and walked back downstairs. The smell of coffee lured me to the cabinets. The damn line rang and rang for what felt like an eternity until, finally, a familiar voice picked up.

"Jasper? That you?"

I sighed. "Dr. Tomb. Thank fuck."

She sighed. "Everything all right?"

"I woke you up, didn't I?"

"No, no, no. Don't go doing all of that. Come on. What's up? I hear it in your voice."

I walked over with my mug of coffee, let Piper in, and kicked the back door closed.

"I've already had two panic attacks since I've been here," I said.

"Two of them?"

"And a nightmare last night. I think. Though I don't remember it."

"And you've been there, what? A week or so?"

"Give or take."

"All right. Well, that's still not as frequent as your attacks were here just a bit ago."

"But it's not as good as I was doing."

"Okay. Walk me through the triggers. What happened when the first one took place?"

I sat down at the kitchen table and walked her through

everything. The issue with my science teacher and that kid over his bike. Going through the shed yesterday. Unlocking it for the first time and smelling the intermingled scents of my parents. As if they had been sitting in there for twelve years, just waiting for me to open the damn door. I didn't mind shedding a few tears. Especially not with Dr. Tomb. She had been a godsend after returning to Vegas from my tour of duty. With specializations in helping vets assimilate back into civilian life, she was the one who recommended that I get Piper.

Among other things.

"All right, are you breathing?" she asked.

I nodded. "Yes, ma'am."

"Good. Keep them even. The first thing you need to do is remember to breathe. I know you don't like that—"

"It's not that I don't like it, it's just—"

"Remember to breathe, Jasper. That's the first thing these attacks rid you of. So, fight against that. The second thing you need to do is hang up with me and get on the phone to the VA in Hartford. I'll put in a recommendation for you the second I get into my office to do some work today. So, you shouldn't have any issues getting a regular therapist to put you on their docket. I know a couple of good ones in that area that work with veterans specifically. I'll make sure to specify them on the recommendation."

"I appreciate that, Doc."

"And one more thing."

"What's that?"

She sighed. "Remember to be kind to yourself. You've stepped back into a place that is filled with triggers you haven't coped with yet. Remember what we said about your military service?"

I nodded. "I was running, not coping."

"Exactly. You ran to the Marines to get away. You didn't

make the Marines some kind of a career goal. Now, you're facing what you were running away from. Be kind to yourself. It's going to take time to sift through all of this. Which is why you need a therapist near you to see once or twice a week."

"Thank you so much for picking up."

"Of course. And until you get these regular appointments going, you can call this number anytime. Okay?"

I ran my hand through my hair. "Yeah, yeah. Thank you. Really."

"All right. I'm going to get myself into the office and get that referral put in. Call the VA. Make that something you do today."

"I will. I promise."

"Good. We'll talk soon."

I went to hang up the phone, but she called to me. "Oh! Jasper!"

I paused. "Yeah?"

"You've worked through some serious things this past week or so. Treat yourself to something nice today. Something that will remind you that you do deserve nice things in your life."

I grinned. "I promise."

I hung up the phone with her and finished my coffee. A new mattress. That could be my treat to myself. I mean, I needed it anyway. So, why not? I finished my coffee and cleaned myself up for the day. I shaved, especially so I didn't have to do it in the morning before work. I led Piper into the cab of the truck before climbing behind the wheel. Then, I set off into town, heading straight for the furniture store.

"Welcome to Olde Farms Furniture! Anything I can help you with?"

I smiled at the kind woman who approached me as I slid my hands into my pockets.

"Got any mattresses by any chance?" I asked.

"Actually, we just had a shipment come in the other day. Looking for any kind in particular?"

"One that doesn't have springs."

"Memory foam, it is."

She led me into a small back room that had some mattresses on display. It was a meager display, but Canaan wasn't known for its massive outlet stores or anything like that. The woman guided me over to a cloud-looking kind of thing and gestured for me to lie on it. When I did, I felt it molding around me, sucking me down and supporting my aching back as I gazed up at the ceiling.

Is this what heaven feels like?

"So, what do you think?" the woman asked.

"Does this require a box spring?" I asked.

"Nope. No springs. Just a platform frame."

She helped me off the mattress, but I didn't want to leave. I wanted to lie back down and close my eyes. That was the kind of mattress I needed. The kind I didn't want to get up from. She pulled me into a corner and showed me all sorts of design imprints on the wall.

"How much?" I asked.

"Mattress is nine-fifty, and if you buy the two-year warranty, the platform frame comes free."

I nodded. "I'll take it, then."

The woman started rounding up the troops, which really just looked like her three boys. It made me grin, though. A family-run business and a mother cracking her whip on the weekend to get her boys to learn the idea of hard work. It reminded me of my own mother, in a way. How she had me helping out around the house at such a young age and out in the yard with Dad, learning all sorts of things. Weed whacking. Mowing the grass. Planting flowers and setting concrete.

"There anything else you're looking to get today?" the woman asked.

I shook my head. "No, I think that's—"

My eyes settled on something shiny on the other end of the room. I made my way for it as the boys hauled the mattress and platform out to the bed of my truck. I crossed the room and stood in front of the television, taking in its sheer size.

"That's a sixty-five-inch flat-screen curve. Just got a couple of 'em in last week."

"You got any wall mounts for it?" I asked.

"Sure do. Though, they're hard to mount. You need to follow the instructions to the letter."

"I can do that."

"I'll add it to your total, then."

I paused. "You got any coffee makers?"

The woman grinned. "I've got every kind you could possibly want."

By the time I left that damn store, I had a mattress, the platform, the television with its wall mount, a very nice coffee maker, and a minifridge to put in my bedroom upstairs.

My next stop was the general store.

I needed more dog food as well as some basics to tide me over until I got to the grocery store. With how piled up the bed of my truck was, I wouldn't be able to buy much. I picked up a few things I liked. A bag of strong coffee and some creamer. I picked up some frozen vegetables and a bit of meat. Some snacks, in case I wasn't up for cooking a decent meal. I snatched a Crock-Pot up, figuring it might make meal prepping a bit easier on me during the harder days.

"Well, hey there, stranger."

It shouldn't have shocked me that I ran into Quinn at the

general store, especially since her parents owned the place. She hugged me from behind, and I chuckled, patting her hands. I turned around, and she started taking things from my arms, carrying them up to the register.

"So, how's your first week home been?"

I sighed. "Uh, it's been a lot."

She nodded. "I can only imagine. Oh, these frozen veggies are on sale. Buy one, get one. So, you can snag another two if you want."

"Thanks. I'll go do that."

"And our steaks are marked down!"

"Appreciate it, Quinn."

"And we have awesome venison jerky!"

I picked up a couple of each item she called out for me, especially since I didn't feel like eating out again for a while. I already felt worn down, tired of people bombarding me. The growing need for space crept up my spine, and I felt myself about to spiral again.

"Deep breaths, Jasper. Just get home first. Okay?" I whispered to myself.

"You need any help?" Quinn asked.

I jumped at the sound of her voice. The steaks tumbled from my arms, and she yelped. Piper appeared at my side, sliding underneath my palm, bracing me for the impending attack. I got checked out as quickly as I could, beads of sweat dripping down my back. And as I carried my small haul to my truck, I tried my best to control my breathing.

Just get home. Just get home. Just get home.

I slammed into my truck and gripped the wheel. Piper curled next to me and moved her snout to my neck. She massaged while I breathed, trying to calm me down enough to drive. As I gazed out the window of my truck, I saw Kent pull up in his own car to the general store before Quinn came rushing out to give him a big hug.

I wonder how close those two are.

I didn't stick around. I needed to get home and unload everything. Get my new bed set up. Get my new coffee maker plugged in. Get this meat in the freezer.

Get myself rooted again.

"Ready to go, Pipes?" I asked.

When she barked in approval, I cranked up the engine of my truck and headed home.

CHAPTER 11

KHLOE

"And there's my long-lost big sister."

I rolled my eyes as Quinn's voice hit my ears.

"Ha. Ha. Ha. Nice one," I said.

"Well, you barely come around the house anymore. So, what else am I supposed to think?" she asked.

"I was there two days ago."

"Yeah, while I was at work."

I shrugged. "Not my fault you want to close the store instead of open it."

"You know I'm not a morning person."

"How do you do that, anyway? Sleep all day, close the general store, then go to the hospital and work your ass off?"

She smiled. "Takes talent, I guess."

"No, you're just crazy."

She laughed. "I brought subs. You hungry?"

"Starving. We can eat in my office. Matt?"

"Already got the front covered. Go enjoy lunch," he said.

I tugged my sister into my office and closed the door behind me. We pulled up chairs to my desk, and I cleared things off. The food she pulled out had my mouth watering.

"Oh, roast beef with pickles and extra mustard. You love me, don't you?" I asked.

"You're damn right, I do. Because that sandwich stinks. I don't know how you eat that stuff," Quinn said.

"You should talk, my office is going to smell like a tuna factory long after you leave," I said.

We tucked into our lunches and fell into a comfortable silence for a few moments.

"Mm, lunch is my treat next time," I said.

"Oh, speaking of treat, guess who came into the store yesterday?"

"Who?"

"Jasper."

I paused. "Oh?"

She nodded. "Mhm. He was picking up a few things. And holy hell, he looked rough."

I decided not to open my mouth about anything. "Well, he's embarking on a high-stress job. One he worked back in a very high-stress city. He's probably just tired. You know, still trying to settle in."

"I don't know. It seemed like more than that, you know?"

She's fishing. "Well, did you ask him?"

"Ask him what?"

"If there was more to it? If he was all right?"

"He just said he was having a rough time settling in."

"And can you blame him after what happened? This is the first time he's been back since his parents died."

She shrugged. "I guess you're right."

I felt my sister staring at me, but I wouldn't betray a damn thing. What happened at Jasper's shed was no one's business unless he wanted to talk about it. Quinn pinned me with a look. She took bites of her sandwich, waiting for me to offer up more information, anything to give her something to talk about later.

Because Quinn was one of the biggest gossips in Canaan.

"So, you're not going to tell me?" she asked.

I swallowed hard. "Tell you what?"

"What you know that I don't?"

"What are you talking about?"

"Oh, come on. Mom and Dad were talking all day yesterday about how you pulled into the driveway before walking off with him."

"So?"

"So? Really? After the hatred you constantly spewed over the years, and you don't think anyone's noticing the time you're spending with him?"

I shrugged. "He wanted help unloading some stuff. I helped him out."

She snickered. "That all you helped him with?"

I pinned her with a glare. "You're toeing a line I don't appreciate."

"Come on. You know something. Spit it out."

I reached for my drink. "What I know is this: Jasper's back in a town that literally killed his parents. He's back in a house he hasn't stepped foot inside in over twelve years. He's back in familiar territory that's doing nothing but bombarding him with painful memories of a life once lived. That, in and of itself, is enough to knock the wind out of anyone."

Her face fell. "I suppose you're right."

"I know I am. Now, leave the poor man alone. He's been through enough."

"It's weird, though."

"What's weird."

"Hearing you defend him."

I shrugged. "I can't hate him forever. It's not good for anyone."

"It's actually nice to see that you guys are friends again."

"What?"

"You know, friends. Hanging out. You helping him. Shit like that. I was beginning to wonder if you'd egg his house or toilet paper his yard."

I laughed. "I'm not that much of a bitch."

"Well…"

"Well, what?"

"I'm not saying you're a bitch. But I am saying you can really hold a grudge when you want to."

I rolled my eyes. "Change the subject."

"That's fine. Been searching for a time to ask you anyway."

"Ask me what?"

"Well, I was thinking. You know, after I saw Jasper at the store. And listening to Mom and Dad talk about how you two went galivanting off to hang out or whatever—"

"I was helping him."

"Yeah, yeah. Anyway. What if we all get together?"

I paused. "What?"

"Yeah. You, me, Jasper, and Kent."

I grinned. "Still on Kent, I see."

Quinn rolled her eyes. "I don't know what you mean."

"Yeah, yeah. You think you hide it well, but I see right through you. I know you've had a crush on that man for a while now."

"Look, it was just an idea. If you don't like it, whatever."

"You don't like being called out, do you?"

"Do you want to get us all together, or not?"

"Quinn and Kent, sitting in a tree."

"Shut up." She growled.

"K-I-S-S—"

"Khloe!"

I put my finger to my lips. "We're in a library. Hush."

She glared at me. "A simple 'no' would've been fine."

"Remember this moment when you want to keep prying for information I don't have."

She sighed. "Deal."

"Now, as for this outing, I don't mind if we do it at all."

"Really?"

I shook my head. "Nope. I think it's a good idea. Especially since Kent and Jasper are working together."

"Wow, I didn't think you'd actually go for it."

"Then why did you ask?"

Quinn shrugged her shoulders. "Figured it was worth a shot."

I nodded. "Anyway, with Jasper looking so rough in public, it might be better if we all meet for dinner somewhere quiet. Like, at my place or something. Might increase our chances of the four of us getting together, so I'm not some weird third wheel while you try and convince Kent to go out with you."

"Hey, you're the one who told me he was into me last year. I've been putting all sorts of signals out there, and he hasn't taken them."

I shrugged. "Maybe you're not putting out the signals he likes, then."

"Or maybe, you were wrong, and he doesn't like me."

I took a bite of my sandwich. "I know that's not true. I see how he looks at you. I see how he smiles at you. Hell, I see how he hugs you. It might be some weird 'bro code' thing or whatever."

"You mean, with him being John's…"

I nodded slowly. "Yeah. With him being John's best friend and all."

Quinn rested her hand against my forearm. "You doing okay?"

"Yeah. I mean, I buried him three years ago. It doesn't

hurt as much to talk about him anymore. Just…reminds me of how lonely it gets sometimes."

"Well, what if we all do dinner at your place? We can all cook together. Or order in some pizza and make it a game night. Bust out some of John's old board games and reminisce."

I sighed. "Well, getting together at my place does make sense. I've got the biggest kitchen."

"Plus, it might be weird trying to do it at Jasper's house."

"And no one wants to go over to Kent's apartment."

Quinn wrinkled her nose. "No, thanks. Can you say 'bachelor city?'"

I grinned. "Man, I know how to out you when I really want to."

"Wait. You—I just meant—fuck!"

I put my finger to my lips again. "Really, Quinn. A library. With kids."

"I'm going to kill you," she grumbled.

"And I want to know exactly how you got Kent to invite you over to his place."

The two of us wrapped up lunch, and I walked Quinn out to her car. I still don't know how she ran the schedule she did or how she found time to harass Kent for his attention. I waved her off before stuffing our trash in the outside trash can. Then, I made my way back inside.

Matt peeked up from beyond a children's book.

"Want me to set you up, too?" I asked.

He chuckled. "Nah. I'm good."

I shrugged. "All right, then. I'll be in my office until two. Then, I'll come relieve you from the front desk."

"I appreciate it."

I walked back into my office and left my door ajar. I sat back down at my desk, though I was more ready to take a nap on the floor. That sub had been way too big. And those chips were impossible to deny. I leaned back and began typing away at the keyboard, answering a few angry emails about overdue book fees, and checking in books from where I sat.

Until my phone ripped me from my trance.

I groaned as I reached down for my purse. I plopped it onto my desk and dug around for my phone. Text after text rolled through, and my gut seized. Was something wrong? Had something happened?

But when I opened the messages, I had to hold back a bark of laughter. The messages were all from Kent.

What the actual fuck? Are you serious?

Did you put her up to this?

I'm going to kill you. Seriously.

I leaned back in my chair and watched as more angry emojis filled my screen. Oh, Quinn wasted no time in going after what she wanted. I giggled to myself as they continued to fill my screen. One, after another, after another. My poor best friend. I knew my sister moved quickly, but this was a bit much. Then again, Kent had no idea how stubborn my sister could be, how relentless she could be once she got her mind attached to something. I typed out a reply.

Just tell her how you feel. That's all she wants.

I dropped my phone back into my purse and slid it off to the side. I had a lot of work to get done before Matthew left for the day, and I didn't need to be spending it trying to talk sense into Kent. It wasn't my fault that Quinn was my sister and I thought they'd be good together. Kent with his reserved nature, and Quinn with her spitfire personality. I mean, the entire town saw it—how he looked at her, how he fawned after her. If he thought he was good at covering it up, he had a rude awakening coming his way.

"Just tell her, you idiot," I murmured.

The more my phone vibrated, the more this dinner

seemed like a good idea. It would get Jasper out of the house for a bit. But not out in public—so he wouldn't get so over-whelmed. This would give Quinn and Kent some one-on-one time. I could easily pull Jasper away to "talk" or "catch up" or "reminisce." And pulling out John's board games he loved to play did sound like a great idea. I hadn't touched those things in over three years.

Yeah. This is a good idea. Way to go, Quinn.

Now, all I had to do was get Jasper on board.

CHAPTER 12

JASPER

M orning. *It's Khloe. I threatened Kent to give me your number. We have an assignment.*

MISSION: GET KENT'S HEAD OUT OF HIS ASS. Everyone knows he's crushing on my little sister. But he won't make a move. Thursday night is the night we strike.

Dinner with you, me, him, and Quinn. My place. Thursday. Seven PM. I'll send you the address.

Oh! And board games. Maybe. Depends if I can handle it. I'll explain later. Here's my address. See you there!

Even through the fog of my sleep, I read her messages perfectly. I didn't expect my phone to be flooded with shit over the course of the night, but I certainly didn't expect the number I didn't recognize to be Khloe's. On the one hand, I should've been upset at Kent for giving out my number. But on the other hand, Khloe had approached him for it.

Did that mean she was warming toward me further?

I had other alerts on my phone as well. A callback from the VA in Hartford. One from my therapist back in Vegas, agreeing to a Skype session to help me make it through. And two messages from guys in my old company asking about coming to visit me at my new place once I got settled in.

But nothing made me feel quite as alive as waking up to texts from Khloe.

I sat up in bed and scrubbed my face with my hands. I had to wake myself up. I certainly wasn't going to be missing dinner with her. So, I put that on my phone calendar first. Thursday night, right at seven. Then, I plugged in her address. According to Google Maps, she didn't live too far away from me. Not even a ten-minute drive.

I had to return a call from the VA in Hartford. The woman who answered assured me that they had spoken with Dr. Tomb, and they had a therapist who had openings in her schedule to see me starting the following week.

I hung up the phone and punched a recurring reminder into my phone calendar. I lived by that thing nowadays. Otherwise, I forgot shit all the time. I tossed my phone to my bed and shuffled into the bathroom, dragging ass to try and wake myself up, especially since I had to get to work in an hour.

But I still found time to call my buddy Ollie that I'd served with.

"What's up, fucker?" he answered on the second ring.

"Not much, dipshit. You?"

We busted each other's balls like old times for a few minutes before Ollie got to the point of his call. "Anyway, I was thinking of coming and visiting. You know, whenever you got settled into your new place. How's Canaan treating you?"

"I mean, I suppose it's going okay despite the fact that I left without a trace."

"Dude, you really need to go easy with that shit on yourself. You were a grieving seventeen-year-old. You fell into depression. It happens."

"Yeah, yeah. I know."

"So, am I free to come visit?"

I buckled my belt. "If you want. I'm in my parents' house for now. Not sure if I'll stay here."

He paused. "Wait, you're staying in your childhood home?"

"It's the only place I had to go up here."

"Are you insane? No wonder you're struggling with shit right now. You're in the mecca for flashbacks. You need to find another place to stay."

"And once I get regular paychecks coming in, I might do that. But for now, I'm in this house."

"Yeah, I'm coming to visit as soon as I can."

I grinned. "Great. I'll vacuum the red carpet."

He barked with laughter. "You're crazy. Okay. I'll take a look at my schedule and put in for some time off. You get any days off?"

"Right now, it's a Monday-to-Friday job, and I don't see that changing. Around here, they reserve weekend duty for those going through the small police academy they've got here."

"All right. I'll give my boss a call."

My phone beeped in my ear. "I gotta go. Got another call. We'll talk soon."

"You know it!"

I quickly tucked the shirt of my uniform in before taking the call. I really should've looked at who was calling first. I assumed it was Kent, wondering where I was or trying to figure out when I'd be in. Instead, though, I got a much different voice.

"Jasper?"

I paused. "Hey, Khloe. Good morning."

"Morning. Did you get my texts?"

I spun around to look at the clock. "Uh, yeah. Yeah, I did. Did you get my text back?"

"No, that's why I was calling."

"Shit. Sorry. It's been a busy morning. Uh, I'm on for Thursday."

"Good! Wonderful. Because it's up to us to finally crack Kent."

"You think this is smart for me to be in on something like this since we don't know each other all that well? And he's my partner at work?"

She laughed. "Yeah, it'll be fine. Don't worry about it. But we need to work on him finally coming out of his shell. My sister knows he likes her. The town knows he likes her. But he's not making a move. It's insane to me."

I chuckled. "I never would have guessed my partner was so willing to die on his own sword. Want me to work on him at work?"

"That would be awesome, Jasper. Can you do that? You know, warm him up for Thursday night?"

"Sure thing. Has he already been invited?"

"Yep."

"Then, he's already going to have an idea of what's going on."

She snickered. "Trust me, Kent is thick-headed. It'll shock you how much so. But my sister is stubborn, and she won't stop until she gets what she wants."

I grinned. "Nice to know things don't change with time."

"You'd be surprised how much really hasn't changed if you think about it."

Like how you feel about me? "Yeah, I suppose you're right."

"Anyway, you get to work before you're late. I have to open up the library. See you Thursday night. And thanks for joining our cause."

My eye twitched. "See you Thursday night."

I hung up the phone as quickly as I could and drew in deep breaths. "Thank you for joining the cause"—that was the only fucking thing I'd heard in basic training. I closed my eyes and placed my hands against the wall. I felt Piper press against my side and nudge my leg. She barked and whimpered, practically begged for attention. And when I dropped my hand down to cling to her coat of fur, she started nuzzling my leg.

Up, and down. Up, and down. Nice, soothing strokes.

"It's okay, Pipes. I got it this time," I said breathlessly.

It took me a couple of minutes to get my head back on straight. But once I did, Piper and I headed out to my truck. She jumped into the bed of it and soaked up the sun while I drove to work. Then, it was simply a matter of switching cars.

"And here I thought you weren't going to show up," Kent said.

I had the good sense to look sheepish. "Coffee's on me? I know I'm shaving it close."

"Nah, you're still three minutes early."

"Which is practically late in military time."

He clapped my back. "Well, it's still early in the regular-person world. But I'll still take you up on the coffee."

"Is that place called Micro's still open?"

"Fuck yeah, it is, and they have the best danishes I've ever tasted."

My mouth watered as we raced toward our destination, and it made me chuckle, seeing how many other police cruisers were lined up ahead of us. I hoped they didn't take all the lemon cream cheese danishes, though.

"So, how was your morning?" Kent asked.

Here we go. "It was all right."

"Get yourself set up at the VA yet?"

"Actually, yes. Monday nights at seven."

"So, you need to be off a bit early?"

I shrugged. "Eh, as long as I'm off right at five, I'll be able to make it."

"That won't be an issue. Chief's a stickler for making sure people are off right on time. We don't do overtime work around here unless it's volunteered for. The county's big about that."

"Sounds good to me."

"Just make sure you run it by him before you leave so he can make a note of it. He likes to keep track of all that kind of stuff."

"Sounds like Chief really takes care of his people."

Kent nodded. "More than most. We're lucky to have him."

Subtlety is for cowards. "So, am I the only one who got that dinner invite this morning?"

He groaned. "Nope. I got it, too. I was wondering if you had actually gotten one, or if this was one of Khloe's contrived ways to get her sister and me alone together."

I shrugged. "I mean, what if it was?"

"Is it?"

"Would it really be such a bad thing to date Quinn? She's a good girl."

Kent stomped on his brakes, and the two of us went jolting toward the front of the car.

"All right, touchy subject," I breathed.

He white-knuckled the steering wheel. "Okay. Look. I get it. People are curious. This entire town likes to talk all the shit they want. But do you really not see the issue with this?"

I shrugged. "The issue with what?"

"She was John's sister in law. And he was as protective of her as if she had been his own flesh."

I furrowed my brow. "And? You were his best friend, so he obviously thought highly of you. It's not like you want to date his wife."

Kent shot me a look. "Never."

I shrugged. "Okay, then. So what's the big deal?"

Kent shook his head. "It's just complicated."

"Sounds like a bunch of bullshit to me. An excuse not to let yourself be happy."

"What? You a shrink now?" he asked.

I sighed. "Look, I know what it looks like to deny yourself happiness. Whatever your reason is, I don't know. Not my place to know unless you want to talk about it. But what I do know is this: Quinn likes you. A lot. And, Khloe is behind you two getting together. And if your best friend is trying to bring you two together in the first place, then what's really holding you back?"

"Welcome to Micro's! What can I get for you this morning?"

Kent grimaced at me, but I knew the groundwork had been laid. He rolled down his window and placed his order, and then I yelled over him to place my own.

"Just think about it and try to have a good time Thursday night. Okay?" I asked.

"Yeah, yeah," he murmured.

Then, we paid for our shit, got our breakfast, and clocked in for the day in the cruiser.

CHAPTER 13

KHLOE

J**asper**: *How's your workday going?*

I furrowed my brow at the text message but decided to respond.

Me: *Quiet, just how I like it. What about yours?*

It didn't take him long to respond at all. Was he on some sort of a break?

Jasper: *Made my first arrest this morning in town. Kent has me on a break to get a snack. Though, I think he's using it as an excuse just to eat.*

I giggled before I leaned back in my chair, deciding to take a break myself.

Me: *Sounds like Kent. The way to his heart really is through his stomach.*

Jasper: *Oh, I laid the groundwork, by the way.*

The floodgates opened, and we ended up texting back and forth throughout the day. The conversation morphed as easily as it used to, and soon we were talking about everything under the sun. Movies. Drama at the general store.

Rumors he'd heard floating around the community since everyone talked to police officers around here. And it felt nice. It felt really nice to be able to talk to him again, to have some sort of access to him again, despite what happened between the two of us.

Though, I wondered if it would flow this easily Thursday evening.

I sighed as I looked at the clock. Already time for my lunch break. I wished Jasper a good day and put my phone up, then felt the grief fill my heart. I closed my eyes, my lower lip quivering as memories of that day came flooding back. John's pale face. His body contorted on the ground. His cheek pressed into the pavement. His chest, unwavering.

"John," I whispered.

The day passed by in a blur after that. Before I knew it, I had to clock out and lock down the library, turn off the lights, and run some errands. I drove on autopilot, lost in the recesses of my mind until a horn honked at me. I jolted back to life and found myself in the middle of the grocery store parking lot, blocking a space someone behind me wanted.

"Sorry! Sorry, I'm sorry."

I waved at them and pulled ahead. I went and parked in back in order to force myself to walk. I needed the fresh air and time to collect myself. And I needed to pick up a few things anyway.

Sorry, Mom and Dad. I need more than a few staples.

This was the first time in years I'd be cooking a full meal for people, and I wanted to be able to impress. I grabbed a small cart and slowly walked the aisles, keeping my eyes out for any sort of inspiration. I didn't want to do anything too easy. So, pot roast in a Crock-Pot was out of the question. Plus, that had been John's favorite, and I didn't need to be conjuring anything like that on Quinn and Kent's evening.

"Khloe?"

I turned around at the sound of the familiar voice.

"Chief Nolan. Hey there," I said.

He came over and gave me a hug before placing his hand on my shoulder like he always did whenever he was holding a conversation with someone.

"How are you doing?" he asked.

I nodded. "I'm okay. I got dinner for four tomorrow night at my place. So, I'm trying to find some inspiration."

"Are you cooking that pot roast of yours?"

I internally winced. "I was thinking about doing something different. Like…"

"Steak?"

"Is that too stereotypical?"

He chuckled. "What if you did a surf and turf? Steak and some shrimp? Or a scampi?"

"Oh, lobster tail. All on the grill."

"There you go. That sounds like a dinner I'd want to enjoy."

"Well, maybe I'll make you a plate and have it delivered."

"A trade-off. My wife's pound cake for a surf and turf dinner."

I moaned. "Oh, Chief Nolan. You add in some of that homemade hot chocolate mix she makes every year for Christmas, and you have yourself a deal."

He squeezed my shoulder. "Great. I'll make sure she knows you're coming by."

He gave me one last hug before walking off, leaving me with a great idea for dinner.

After thirty minutes of finding all I needed, I walked back out to my car. The drive home felt a little less daunting, and I got home with enough daylight to unload the groceries from the car. I unpacked everything and got the steaks marinating. After everything else was put away, I paused.

I let my emotions guide me. Tonight would be rough. But

it would be the first rough night in eight or nine months. A record in my world. I moved down the hallway of our ranch-style home, coming to the first room on my left. My hand settled on the doorknob. I felt tears rushing my eyes as my hand began to tremble. And when I tossed the door open, John's scent filled my nostrils.

"Oh, God," I whispered.

I flipped the light on and looked at the room, filled to the brim with John's things. After he passed, I just moved his stuff in here. I didn't have the heart to go through it and purge it. As my eyes settled onto his board games, I felt that all-too-familiar ache in my heart.

Maybe it's time to move on now, Khloe.

The thought took my breath away. But it didn't hurt. It just shocked me. The idea of actually going through this stuff. Of actually being ready to let go of him. I quickly closed the door and squeezed my eyes shut and shook my head.

"You don't have to have the answers now," I whispered to myself.

And yet, the only thing that had changed in three years was Jasper's presence. Was he somehow helping me to grieve? Helping me to get past things? And if he was, what did that say about how much I loved John?

"You're a terrible person," I choked out.

CHAPTER 14

JASPER

I sat in bed with my laptop in my lap, waiting for Dr. Tomb to call. This would probably be our last call, so I wanted to make it a good one. I had myself prepared to talk about some heavy topics, things that had been floating around in my mind. But I also had some good things to talk about.

Like dinner tonight.

My laptop started ringing, and I quickly picked up the call. The video buffered, but I clearly saw Dr. Tomb on the other end. I cleared my throat and slid my hands down my shirt. I wasn't sure if she'd notice that I had already gotten dressed up for the evening. But I was prepared to unpack everything if she—

"Well, well, well. You look nice tonight, Mr. Willem."

I grinned. "I was wondering if you'd notice."

"I figured I'd catch you in your uniform still. What's the occasion?"

"Well, I've got a dinner tonight to go to."

"Oh? A nice dinner?"

I snickered. "Yeah, you could say that."

"Well, why don't you talk about it?"

We spent the next hour going over what I'd done the past few days since our last call and how I'd been getting on at work. She knew that it was always easier for me to manage my anxiety while working, which really didn't make much sense since the job could be hectic. But for some reason, focusing on what I was doing when I was on patrol was always easier than simply navigating the world around me.

As we were winding up the conversation, I thanked the doctor for all the help she'd given me the past couple of years.

She grinned. "Have fun at your dinner, Mr. Willem. And remember: your past is only a harness if you allow it to be. This might be a good time to talk with Khloe about what happened all those years ago and give her some answers."

"I know."

"So, if it comes up, don't shy away from it."

"I won't."

"Good. Good to hear. You've been a wonderful patient."

I barked with laughter. "You're a terrible liar."

"Goodbye, Mr. Willem."

I hung up the Skype call, and I didn't feel as weighed down as I usually did. I closed my laptop and slid out of bed, ready to get my ass on the road. I had fifteen minutes to get there before I was late.

"All right, Jasper. You got this," I murmured to myself.

I decided not to take Piper with me, especially since Khloe seemed jumpy around her. I brushed Piper on the back before leaving her enough food and water. Then, I headed for my truck. The drive was easy, but it shocked me how tucked away she was in the woods. I passed by acres of trees and empty farmland before coming to a mailbox on the right-hand side of the road boasting of the house number I was looking for.

"I guess this is it," I whispered.

I turned down the gravel driveway and inched my way back into the woods. The trees were thick, and even though the sky was filled with stars, not a single shred of light penetrated the canopy. This was where Khloe lived? I didn't like her being all the way out here by herself. In the woods. Vulnerable. Isolated.

I pulled up to the house, and my headlights landed on the structure. It was a quaint little one-story place that looked more like a cottage than anything else. It made me grin, too. The house suited Khloe. Charming, but not decadent. The white trim and the navy blue wooden side paneling looked beautiful against the nighttime of the woods.

But as I continued scanning the property, my eyes landed on a tarp.

Not just the tarp, though, but the shining red thing underneath it. It seemed out of place, especially underneath an awning made for a car. I turned off my truck and slipped out. The world fell almost pitch-black around me until my movement caused some lights to kick on. I walked up to the tarp and lifted it up, taking stock of the bright red thing underneath it.

And when I saw the motorcycle, my eyes widened.

It must be her late husband's.

Jealousy ripped through my body. Despite me not having a reason to be jealous, I felt it anyway. I dropped the tarp and pulled it down, covering the rest of the bike up. Khloe always deserved to have love. To find a love for the ages. And I hadn't been there to give it to her.

I didn't have a right to hold that against her.

"It's a nice bike, isn't it?"

I jerked around and saw Khloe standing on the front porch.

"I'm sorry. It just caught my eye."

"Come on in. I've got a bottle of wine already open," she said.

She motioned with her head, then walked back inside. I sighed heavily, wondering if I had already put my foot in it. She didn't sound angry. But Khloe also wasn't one to showcase her anger. Well, she *hadn't* been one to do it—she sure as hell did it when I first got back into town.

The Khloe you know is from twelve years ago. She's different now.

"Fuck," I groaned.

I made my way into her house, and it made me smile. Damn it, this place suited her so much. The navy from the outside of the house carried on into the inside. The walls were navy, and the crown molding was white. The baseboards were white. Even the hardwood floors had a bright tint to them. To my left, the living room, with a bright blue accent wall where the television was mounted against its surface. To my right, a hallway, with the navy blue carrying all the way down its expanse toward a door at the end of it.

"Keep walking forward. Kitchen's through here," Khloe said.

I flickered my eyes along the walls. And while I saw nails embedded into studs, there were no pictures hanging on them. I furrowed my brow as I heard liquid being poured. I emerged into the kitchen, and there were a couple of stools to my right, curving around with the bar. The dining room table was a beautiful mahogany wood, complete with matching chairs and a small crystal chandelier hanging from the ceiling.

I couldn't get over how this place matched Khloe so well.

"John let me decorate however I wanted," she said.

I felt the glass of wine press into my palm as she stood in front of me.

"I can definitely see that," I said. "It looks like you."

"He was about as much of a man as any other man. Didn't give a damn about outside appearances. Could've lived in his own filth, if you let him. And he was very attached to that bike out there. Always out there, tinkering with it whenever he could."

"He sounds like a good man."

She sipped her wine. "He was."

I paused. "Listen, if you don't want to—"

"When you told me you were sorry about my loss at that Friday event? I figured Kent had told you something. And for a while, I was upset about that. What happened to John is my business. It happened to me, and no one else had a right to tell you about that."

"I know. I'm sorry."

"It's nothing for you to be sorry about. John was a good man. You would've liked him."

"I'm sure I would have."

"Did Kent tell you how he died?"

CHAPTER 15

KHLOE

I held my breath, waiting for him to tell me all he knew. Because for all *I* knew, this town had filled him in on everything. I didn't want this night to be about my tragedy, because the focus was Kent and Quinn. But Jasper had gazed at that bike for far too long. And I knew Jasper. Well, maybe not as well as I once knew him. But I knew he'd be asking himself about that bike all night, wondering about it, distracting him from the purpose of this dinner.

"Yes, Kent told me what happened to him."

I nodded slowly. "Great."

"If it makes you feel any bet—"

"It won't. But I guess I shouldn't have expected any differently from Kent. He was probably doing it to try and protect me, or explain something, or whatever it was he had on his mind. So, I'll fill in the blanks."

"You really don't have to."

I took another sip of my wine. "Maybe I want to?"

He nodded. "Then, I'm all ears."

I sighed. "I actually met the bike before I met John. He was attending the community college I enrolled in, and I saw it parked in one of the back-parking lot spaces. I went over to admire it and ended up being late for class."

He grinned. "Sounds like something you'd do."

"Ha. Ha. Ha. Anyway, I came back out to look at the bike again, but it was gone. I figured that was that. But it kept showing up. Every morning, at that exact same time. In that exact same spot."

"So, you kept staring at it?"

"For a while. Until I figured out that its owner was in my class."

He chuckled. "What class?"

"Intro to Economics. I failed it in spectacular fashion. Probably because I didn't do much with my tutoring sessions other than stare at him."

"Why did you stare at him during yo—?" Then, I saw it click in his stare. "Oh."

I nodded. "Yeah."

"John was your…?"

I sighed. "Yes, John was my professor. And before you get any sort of weird 'sixty-year-old man hitting on an eighteen-year-old girl' vibes, he was only twenty-seven. Just starting his teaching career."

"Not a great way to start it."

I shot him a look. "Maybe this was a bad idea."

"No, no, no, no. Hey. I just—I'm sorry."

I went to turn away from him before I felt something warm against my skin. It stopped me in my tracks, and the second I saw his hand wrapped around my wrist, my heart stopped. His touch felt grand. I drew in a deep breath as I slowly looked over my shoulder. My gaze caught his as his Adam's apple bobbed. I practically heard him swallow as I turned a bit back toward him.

"I'm sorry," Jasper said.

I nodded softly. "It's okay. A lot of people judged."

"I didn't mean to—"

"A lot of people thought a lot of things, Jasper. That he had forced himself on me. That he was the reason I dropped out of school. But, if anything, John was the reason I found my feet underneath me again."

He said nothing, only nodded.

"Jay, you leaving devastated me. Not hearing from you at all destroyed me. I went through my senior year in a haze. I quit the volleyball team."

"Khlo, I'm so sorry."

"Can you just listen? Because I've been waiting a long time to tell you this."

He squeezed my hand. "Yeah. Go ahead."

I drew in a deep breath. "By the time I graduated, my grades had slipped. I had a 2.4 GPA and no hope of Cal Tech. Mom wanted me to take a year off. Get some counseling. But Dad wanted me to pull myself up by my bootstraps and keep on trucking. So, I compromised. I stayed here with them and enrolled in the local community college. I actually avoided taking classes with him after that first semester just so he could take me out on a date."

I felt Jasper's grip growing tighter as I fell back into the memories.

"He helped me forget, Jay. He made me smile. And laugh. And our dates were always punctuated with a ride on the back of that bike of his. When I felt trapped by school, he encouraged me to seek out other avenues. When I found out that the library was hiring, he encouraged me to put in an application. And when I got the job, he stood by me against my parents while they fought me every step of the way."

"He sounds like a great man."

Tears rushed to my eyes. "He was, Jasper. He was the best kind of man. And I loved him with everything I was capable of. He cheered me on. Provided me what I needed. And he never once expected me to be anything other than the broken girl he met that first semester in community college."

I closed my eyes as I pulled my hand away from his.

"And then, he died. One morning, during his routine run. He left for his run, I had breakfast prepared for when he got back. And then, he never came home."

"Khlo, I'm so fucking sorry."

I finally turned toward him and found Jay with watery eyes.

"I buried him three years ago. But I don't think that hurt will ever go away," I said.

He shook his head slowly. "It won't. But it'll get easier to live with."

"Maybe so. But that should fill in all the gaps of my history with John. Because tonight is about Kent and Quinn. I don't want anything distracting us from that."

"Will you tell me more about him later?"

His question shocked me. "What?"

He took a step toward me. "Will you tell me more about him later?"

I nodded softly. "If you want."

"I would like to know more about the man who stepped up when I failed you."

I nearly choked at his words, but before I could say anything else, he slipped away from me, moving his way into the kitchen. I let out a shaky sigh, then tossed back the rest of my wine.

Holy hell, I'd need much more if to get through tonight.

"So, what's for dinner?" Jasper asked.

"Steak, lobster tail, whipped potatoes, and grilled vegetables," I said.

"Oh, that sounds fantastic."

"I was going to strike up the grill, but I'm thinking about pan-frying the steaks since they're filets."

His eyebrows rose. "Filet mignon for dinner tonight. This must be important."

"Oh, yes. Our mission is very important. I don't want anything impeding on it, either."

"Nothing impeding. Got it," he said.

"Good. Now, would you like to help? Because I could use some help chopping up all these damn vegetables."

We danced around one another in the kitchen, and I found that I didn't hate it. I hadn't cooked with anyone in a very long time. Especially since the last time I'd cooked with someone, it was with John.

"Everything okay?" Jasper asked.

I shook my head. "Yeah, yeah. I'm good. Just waiting for this pan to heat up."

"Pretty sure it's done."

I looked down at the melted butter and snickered.

"Time for the steaks," I said.

A knock came at the door, and I motioned for Jay to go get it. The second Quinn and Kent's laughter filled the house together, my head snapped over. Had they arrived together? Or just pulled up at the same time? Jasper came around the corner and shrugged, which literally gave me nothing to go on.

"Holy shit! Something smells fantastic in here," Kent said.

"The important guests have arrived," Quinn said.

I peeked over my shoulder at Jay and watched him peel the potatoes.

"So, did you two come together? Or pull up together?" he asked.

"Jasper," I hissed.

"What? You know you're thinking it."

"I mean, how long has Jasper been here alone with you?" Quinn asked.

I shot her a look. "Quinn."

She shrugged. "We pulled up together. But we may or may not have been talking outside for a bit before Kent kindly ushered me up the porch steps."

I groaned and rolled my eyes as Kent and Quinn burst out laughing.

The more they laughed together, the closer they grew. Dinner was filled with uproarious sounds, to the point where Quinn was practically leaning on Kent for support. And he was quick to wrap his arm around her. I liked the sound of the two of them together. Listening to them talk. Watching Kent cradle her close. I knew he'd take care of my baby sister. And that was something she deserved.

Though, I could've done without Jasper practically shoving Quinn into Kent's lap.

"We could play spin the bottle," Jasper said.

He came up behind me and slid some dishes into the sink.

I shot him an incredulous look, but when Jasper started laughing, I found myself laughing along with him.

"Hey, you two. Sounds like you're having too much fun in here," Kent said.

"Yeah! Since when are dishes funny?" Quinn asked.

Jasper quickly stepped away, and I drew in a deep breath.

"So, are you guys up for a game or something? I've got one last bottle of wine for the night," I said.

Kent held up his hand. "If I have any more, I won't be able to drive."

"And I do have to work tomorrow," Quinn said.

"All right. Well, let me walk you two to the door," Jasper said.

I quirked an eyebrow at him, and he winked back. I felt my heart skip a beat as he walked them to the door. But the second the door closed, he rushed back into the kitchen.

"Come on, come on, come on," he murmured.

He grabbed my hand and started tugging me toward the door.

"What? What's going on?" I asked.

"I may or may not have pep-talked Kent in the corner earlier about kissing Quinn tonight," he whispered.

"Why are we whispering?"

"I don't know."

"Well, you started it."

I looked over at him and saw him smiling brightly, igniting those beautiful eyes that had made my heart flutter as a teenager. I smiled back at him, feeling at ease in his presence. But when he turned his stare back out the window, I followed in kind.

Only to see Kent's head dip toward Quinn's.

"Yes!" I exclaimed.

Jasper put his finger to his lips and started laughing.

"They're going to hear you all the way from here," he said.

I stood up and danced around, rejoicing as they kissed outside. Yes! The dinner had been a success. I pumped my fists in the air as Jasper fell apart in laughter. And for a moment, it felt like old times. Our old plans. Our old antics.

Our old ways.

CHAPTER 16

JASPER

"You know Khloe saw that kiss, right?"

"It almost didn't happen."

"Oh, come on. You know you'd been thinking about it all night. You were practically playing footsies with her underneath the table at dinner."

"Maybe," was all he'd say, though the ear-to-ear grin said it all.

"Is that her? Why are you smiling at her phone?"

"Maybe," he said again.

"Kent has a girlfriend. Kent has a girlfriend."

"Dude, shut up."

All morning, I busted his balls like a good partner should.

Kent sighed. "She's amazing, isn't she?"

The look on my partner's face when he said those words gave me pause. I looked over at him as I ate my sandwich, since we were wolfing down lunch in the cruiser. I saw him staring at his phone and peeked over his shoulder. And the text I saw made me grin.

I saw Quinn's name, with a bunch of kissy faces filling a text message screen.

"She's a good one, yeah," I said.

Kent started typing back to her. "I've liked Quinn for so long. I mean, going on two or so years now. It killed me to do what I thought was right. I mean, seeing her all the time and not being able to touch her just…"

I sat there, waiting for him to finish that statement.

"Do you know what it's like to stare at the woman you're in love with for months on end and feel like you can't touch her?" he asked.

Actually, yeah. "Must be rough, man."

He sent off the text. "It is. And now, I finally get to take her in my arms and kiss her and do all that stuff I've wanted to do for so long."

I smiled. "Well, you could have had this a long time ago, you know. Khloe's been angling at it for a while, it seems."

"I'm an idiot. I get it."

"No, you were just being stubborn. A stubborn gentleman. You wanted what was best for Quinn and her reputation in town. There's nothing wrong with that. And now? You get to start making it up to her."

His phone dinged with a text, and he chuckled. He tilted the phone over to me, and I practically barked with laughter.

You and me. Tomorrow night. I'm coming over to help you clean that nasty bachelor pad you've got. You can cook dinner to make it up to me. See you around five!

"Oh, man. You're in for a ride with her," I said.

"Guess I get the pleasure of making up a lot now," Kent said, grinning.

"Love looks good on you, you know."

He snickered as he slid his phone back into his pocket.

"It looks good on you, too," he said.

I furrowed my brow. "What?"

"Time to get back on the road."

I stuffed my sandwich back in its bag. "Wait, wait, wait. What did you mean by that?"

"Time for us to clock back in, partner!"

I narrowed my eyes at him as he pulled away from the curb. As I stared at him, we started driving down the road, making our usual after-lunch rounds that had become routine for us. I decided to shrug off the statement. At least, for now.

But I'd get back around to it.

"Oh, by the way. The library's having a story time. I thought we could stop in and say hi to the kiddos. They get a kick out of it," Kent said.

I nodded. "Fair enough. What time is it?"

"In a few minutes. Just wanted to give you a heads-up. You know, like I promised."

I rolled my eyes. "Yeah. A few minutes' heads-up. Thanks for that."

"Don't act like you don't want to see her. ."

I shot him a look, and he threw his head back with laughter. Then, we made our way over to the library. Piper stayed by my side the entire time as we walked in. And I got to witness yet another one of her wonderful Matthew introductions.

"I bet if everyone closes their eyes, he'll reappear before we know it. You guys ready to close your eyes?" Khloe asked.

I watched at the kids put their hands over their faces as Kent, Piper, and I took up our posts against the wall. Khloe looked over at me and nodded. But the cheeky grin on her face made my heart flutter in my chest. Kent nudged me, and I nudged him back. I didn't need him getting any ideas. I wasn't in love with Khloe, and she wasn't in love with me.

We were merely trying to get a feel for one another again after all these years.

"All right, everyone. Now, say the magic word," Khloe said.

"Merry Christmas!"

"Bippity boppity boo!"

"Trick or Treat!"

"Please?"

Every kid shouted a different magic word, and I had to put my hand over my mouth to keep from laughing out loud. I even saw Khloe suppressing her own laughter as Matthew jumped out from around the corner. The kids opened their eyes and cheered for him as he sat down in a chair. Then, he sat a massive children's book on his knee to start reading to them.

Khloe came and took up a position beside me.

"You ever read this book?" she whispered.

I shook my head. "I don't recognize it, no."

"Oh, *Goodnight Moon* was a favorite of mine."

"If everyone is ready, I can begin," Matthew said.

When I looked over at him, he was staring directly at Khloe and me. Whoops.

"I'm an officer of the law. I'm always ready," I said.

Khloe giggled. "Ready."

Matthew chuckled. "All right, then."

The book was really sweet. A child saying good night to everything in his room, including his mother and the moon. I saw why it was Khloe's favorite. She used to do that all the time with her dolls and stuffed animals. Though, she'd never admitted that to anyone. Ever. I kept stealing glances at her as Matthew kept reading through the book and entrancing the children.

Then, once the story wound down, I drew in a deep breath.

"Why don't you come over tonight for some dinner?" I asked without much thought.

Her eyes whipped up to mine. "What?"

"Dinner. You know, that thing you eat?"

She swatted me playfully. "Sure, I could eat. What's the occasion?"

"Well, Kent is going to be preoccupied with your sister. And I figured I'd do a little more shed snooping if I'm feeling up for it. I figured I could entice you over for food, we could catch up—."

She placed her hand on my arm. "Whatever you need, Jay. I'll help you out, okay?"

She hadn't called me that in years. No one had. I never let anyone truncate my name like that. Hearing it fall from her lips after all these years made my heart seize in my chest.

"I appreciate it. Thank you," I said.

Kent kept shooting me glances for the rest of the day, but I ignored them. I kept running down in my head what I needed to get from the store to cook a decent enough dinner. I was no chef, but I knew my way around a few recipes. Lasagna with a salad. A nice pot roast. I was good with ribs. I needed a couple of days to prep those, however.

"So, what's on the menu for tonight?" Kent asked.

I grinned. "I'm thinking about doing a nice Southern meal."

"A Southern meal? With all that grease?"

"Eh, depends on what you cook. I'm thinking macaroni and cheese, some cornbread, oven-baked chicken, and potato salad."

"Nice. Can I come?"

"I'll make you a plate and bring it over later. How's that sound?"

He chuckled. "You mean, there's going to be a 'later' for you?"

I cut my eyes to him. "I didn't invite Khloe over to screw around with her."

He held his hands up in surrender. "Just busting your balls, man."

"Fair enough," I said. "So, what's the occasion?"

"For dinner?"

He nodded. "Yep."

"Well, we still have a lot of catching up to do. She opened up to me a lot about John before you and Quinn came over for dinner last night. I figured I owed her at least a bit of opening up myself. Answering questions she might have."

"What did she tell you about John?"

I shrugged. "How they met. How long they were together. Rides on his motorcycle."

"He fucking loved that thing."

I heard a waver in Kent's voice and patted him on the shoulder.

"It's time she had answers, and I plan on giving those to her tonight. Any questions she's got."

He nodded. "I appreciate that. She's wanted them for a long time."

"Yeah. I know."

I decided not to tell Kent about anything else. Because while I was glad my friendship with Khloe seemed to be on the mend, part of me hoped we could be more than that. Eventually. Sometime in the future. But tonight definitely wasn't the night for that.

"All right, time to head back to the station," Kent said.

I paused. "Wait, what?"

"Yep. Time for you to go home."

"It's only four-thirty."

"Uh-huh."

"And the station's just up the block."

"Yep."

"Why am I being let off early?"

He chuckled. "Because you need to do some grocery

shopping. And don't forget the fresh donuts. Go by the general store and get them straight from her father. She fucking loves those things."

I smiled. "That man always made the best donuts. It's nice to know he's finally selling them now."

"Exactly. And have fun tonight. But, you know, not too much fun."

I nodded. "I plan on having the exact right amount of fun that respects Khloe and makes her smile."

"And you say you're not in love."

CHAPTER 17

KHLOE

As I stood on the porch, I felt nervous about being there. Which was insane, given the fact that I'd been to this house so many times. Still, I raised my knuckles and knocked softly against the door, readying myself for whatever the night had in store for me.

Well, for us.

The first sound I heard was Piper barking, then the skittering of her feet along the floors. That high-pitched whistle rose behind the door, however, and the dog stopped. Amazing, the training Piper had. Very telling of the time Jasper had spent with her.

But when the door opened, all thoughts of Piper fell to the wayside.

"Hey there, Khloe. Thanks for coming. I just need to pull the chicken out, and dinner is all set."

I had to force my jaw to stay in its place. Even so, my mouth still watered. Not because of the smells coming from the kitchen, either. Jay looked outstanding. With his dark-wash jeans and his tight button-down shirt, I saw the ripples of muscles I didn't even know him to have. His clean-shaven face was accented with a soft shadow. The piercing green of his eyes stopped my heart in my chest. There was a churning in my pelvis, in my gut, and as my eyes slid along the swell of his chest, I felt heat gather between my legs.

"Khloe?"

I cleared my throat. "Yes, sorry. Long day at the library."

"Well, come in and take a load off. I've got wine."

He ushered me into the house, and I brushed by him. The heat of his body, alone, caused my gut to jump. But the smell of his cologne made my nipples pucker. It seemed as if my nonexistent sex drive had been awakened, and I felt my mouth running dry.

I need a distraction. Something. Anything.

"Hello there, Piper. How are you? Oh, come here. Hey there, fluffy puppy."

I bent down, and Piper came rushing toward me. I focused my attention on her as Jay stood at his perch, watching us. I scratched behind her ears as she sat in front of me. She scooted a bit closer, then laid her snout against my shoulder.

"Aw, you're not so bad. Such a good puppy. There's a good girl."

I even chanced a kiss against her coat of fur, which elicited a soft whimper from the golden retriever.

"And here I thought you didn't like animals," Jay said.

I stood. "Ah, well. Piper's a good girl when she's not trying to jump on me."

Piper answered with a resounding bark before nuzzling her nose against my leg.

"Here, let me take your coat," he said.

His fingertips slid against my skin as he removed my coat from my shoulders. Electricity sizzled down my spine, and I tried my best to ignore it. I was here for answers. Not anything else. I deserved answers to my questions, so I had to stay in a frame of mind to ask them.

"And a glass of wine for you," he said.

I turned around. "Did you have this on standby or something?"

He smiled. "A man never reveals his secrets. Here. Mine's in the kitchen still."

I followed him into the kitchen and sat down at the table, right where one of the plate settings were. The table was full of amazing food. Cornbread and macaroni and cheese. Mashed potatoes, and what looked like a homemade gravy.

"Are those turnip greens?" I asked.

"Collard greens, I think is what they're called. But yes," Jay said.

I watched him slide the chicken out, and the kitchen filled with a wondrous lemon scent.

"Wow, you really went all out," I said.

He chuckled. "I think I went a bit overboard, yes. But that just means you can take yourself a plate home."

"And with how good this smells, I just might."

He sat down after placing the chicken where it needed to be. And his glistening forehead made me wonder what else on his body was glistening with sweat. I swallowed hard before taking a long pull of wine. I'd need a lot of it to get through tonight.

Okay, Khloe. Settle down. You have questions, he has answers.

"Khloe, I want to start off by saying—"

"Why did you never call?" I blurted out, cutting him off.

He blinked. "I guess we can hop right into it."

I nodded. "I'd like that, actually. It's been a struggle, not asking you up until this point."

"Well, then it's about time you had your answers."

I watched him fill my plate with food before he filled his. A scoop of everything, with gravy drizzled all over. His hands trembled, and I saw the fear in his eyes. My heart went out to him. It really did. As hard as this was for me, I could only imagine how hard it was for him.

So, I offered my hand to him.

"Talk to me, Jay. What happened?" I asked.

His eyes dropped to my hand before he took it, and I felt his pulse racing against my fingertips as they settled against his wrist.

"When I left with my aunt, the flight back was hard. She couldn't stop crying. She couldn't stop reminiscing. And it tore me apart. She always wanted to talk, and I just wanted her to shut up."

I nodded, but I didn't interject.

"I slipped into a terrible depression when we got to Vegas. I slept all the time. I barely ate."

"I'm so sorry, Jay."

"I should have called. I need you to understand that I know I should have called. I just…"

"I know that kind of depression. The kind that makes even breathing a chore."

"I barely passed most of my classes. Some Ds. Some Cs. My GPA dropped to a two-point… something. I mean, I tanked."

I snickered. "Yep. I get that, too."

He sighed. "Career Day happened at school, and I almost didn't go. But my aunt forced me to. So, I did. And the Marines had a booth set up. I mean, I didn't have a chance at college by that point. So, I figured, why not?"

"So, you enlisted."

He nodded. "Yep. I did. I went to basic training that summer and was shipped out into an area no eighteen-year-old boy should ever have to witness. Or any boy, for that matter."

"Where were you?"

"I was stationed at Camp Dwyer in Afghanistan. Supposedly, it wasn't a very active area at the time. So, we should've been safe. But I went out on patrol with my guys one day and—"

I hung on to his every word as he squeezed my hand.

"It's okay. I'm right here, Jay," I said softly.

He sighed. "We were out on patrol. Our convoys rolled right over a set of IEDs. I watched the explosions. Saw the vehicles just shoot up into the air."

I held back tears. "My God."

"I lost everyone. Everyone I had befriended on that patrol. Soaring through the air felt like slow motion. Like, in the movies. I couldn't save any of them. They all just—just bled out around me. I held all of their hands. Just—pulled them as close as I could get them, so they knew they weren't alone."

I shot up from my chair and pulled him in for a hug.

"I gotcha, Jay. I'm right here. It's okay. You're safe."

"I see them every night. I can't—I can't stop smelling the —the-the-the—"

I closed my eyes as I felt his tears dripping against my shoulder.

"I'm so sorry, Jay," I whispered.

"I should've called. I'm so fucking sorry for not calling," he said breathlessly.

"It's okay. It's done. It's past. And we're here now. It's going to be okay."

"I was so in love with you for years, Khlo."

I paused. "What?"

He sniffled. "I was. I know it's pathetic to admit now. But God, there wasn't a fucking moment growing up where you didn't steal my breath away."

I held him out with my hands. "Are you serious?"

"I know it's shitty to bring up now. But you should know."

I gazed into his watery eyes. "I was in love with you, too, Jay."

He furrowed his brow. "You were?"

I snickered. "Yeah. Big-time."

He cupped my cheek. "All this time."

I closed my eyes. "We were both idiots, Jay. Big, young, dumb idiots."

I clung to his shirt, feeling him slowly move closer to me. His breath against my lips gave me a taste of him. The way he held my cheek made my heart skip a beat. All this time, he had loved me. I shut my brain down. I closed all logic on the situation. And when his lips touched mine, nothing could have prepared me for how wondrous he tasted.

"Oh, Khlo," he groaned.

His arms cloaked my back. He pulled me in as I wrapped my arms around him. My head fell off to the side, and his tongue slid along mine, pulling me along for the ride. My knees weakened. My legs quivered. Electricity surged through my body, jolting me alive for the first time in years. Our teeth clattered together as he stood up and gripped my hips. I jumped, and he bent down, allowing me to wrap my legs around him before he carried me toward the stairs.

I devoured him as he walked up the steps. I sucked on his lower lip, pulling growls from his throat. My back pressed against the wall as his hands journeyed along my body, massaging and gripping, exploring in all the ways I'd wanted as a teenage girl. I gasped as his lips slid down my neck. He nibbled my pulse point and massaged my clothed breasts. I rocked against him, wanting nothing more than friction to take us both away, to carry us off into a land of happiness we both deserved.

"Jay," I moaned.

"Oh, fuck, Khlo," he grunted.

And as a door slammed open, he pulled me away from the wall.

My back fell to a mattress before he crashed against me. I heard the seams of our clothes tearing as we practically ripped them from each other's bodies. My eyes rolled back as his lips wrapped around my pert nipples, his tongue lapping against my skin. My pussy was soaked , ready for his intrusion as his cock fell against my thigh, pulsing and thickening and leaking for me.

"Now. Jay, please."

"I want more of you. All of you."

I reached for his cock. "I can't wait a second longer. Please, Jay."

He groaned as I stroked him. I felt him growing in my hand as I positioned him at my entrance. My eyes found his, and he grinned. Then, his lips captured mine once more. His body came forward, and I felt him pierce me, filling me up as he slid against my walls. I clung to him tightly, wrapping my legs around his hips. And as he bottomed out inside me, my head fell back to the pillow.

"Holy shit," I whispered.

He started slow, softly rocking, kissing my neck and my shoulders. He massaged my tits and tugged my nipples to painful peaks. I felt my juices dripping down below us as he teased me, his tightly wound curls tickling my swollen clit. My toes slid down the backs of his legs, and my nails curled into the chiseled muscles of his back. I felt every part of him moving against me, working for our mutually beneficial pleasure.

"Faster," I whispered.

He growled in response as he picked up the pace.

"Harder," I moaned.

He grunted as the sounds of skin slapping skin echoed off the corners of the room.

"More," I groaned.

He sank his teeth into my neck and marked me as my body quaked underneath him.

He slipped my leg over his shoulder, opening me up more. He rose up, giving me the perfect view of the thick rings around his abs. He gripped my hips and pulled me closer. I felt him slide farther into my body as my jaw unhinged. He pounded into me, filling me and growling out my name as the pleasure choked off my ability to speak.

"Khlo. Yes. Holy fuck. All this time. Oh, shit."

My eyes rolled into the back of my head. My toes curled with the force of my orgasm. My back arched and my body released, drenching him in my juices. The sound of us colliding together shot fire through my veins, and the sound of my name falling from his lips brought my heart back to life.

"Jay. Yes. Fuck. Don't stop. Don't stop."

And as I collapsed against the bed, he came along with me, blanketing my body as his cock filled me to the brim, marking me as if I had been his own all along.

CHAPTER 18

JASPER

W aking up with Khloe in my arms the next morning was something I could have never expected from our dinner. With the food cold downstairs and the stale scent of wine hanging in the air, I felt her nuzzle even closer to me. She turned over and sighed, her soft snores quickly falling from her lips again. As I gazed into her angelic face, I tucked a strand of hair behind her ear.

"I love you," I whispered.

Everything about this was so new to me. Having her here. Naked. Her gorgeous curves keeping me warm all night. Not only that, though, last night was the first night I'd been nightmare-free since coming home from that deployment. I smiled at the thought. Who would've thought a few good rounds of sex was all it would take to keep my mind quiet?

I had a feeling it wasn't just the sex, though.

Thank you for doing your part for your country, beautiful.

I snorted at the thought, and I felt Khloe jump.

"What in the world are you laughing at this early?" she murmured.

I chuckled. "Sorry, beautiful."

I kissed her softly on her cheek before she pulled the covers over her head.

"Is the sun even up yet?" she murmured.

"Barely," I said.

"Then, I'm barely up. Shush, so I can sleep."

I grinned. "I can do that."

As she nuzzled that soft ass of hers against my pelvis, I slipped my arm around her. I pulled her close, sliding underneath the covers with her. I buried my face into the crook of her neck and kissed her softly as she sighed and yawned.

"You're not helping," she said flatly.

I kissed her shoulder. "All right, all right. I'm done. I promise."

This felt an awful lot like happiness. The weight off my shoulders. A good night's sleep. My heart, beating with a need for more of life. I wasn't sure I trusted it, though. Everything good in my life always crumbled. From my parents to the guys on that patrol to my friendship with Khloe.

That's on the mend, though.

I snorted again, and she groaned.

"If you're going to keep making noise, at least get me some coffee," she grumbled.

"How about I just make us breakfast?" I asked.

"Yes. Out of bed with you. Give me five more minutes of sleep."

I chuckled. "Of course, beautiful."

I kissed her shoulder once more before sliding out of bed. I didn't know if this was what happiness felt like, but I'd grab it with both hands and hang on for as long as I could. I pulled on some pajama pants and a T-shirt, then headed downstairs. I needed to put up dinner before starting breakfast, and Piper needed to go out.

But every part of me wanted to go back upstairs and wake Khloe up the right way.

Focus. The woman needs coffee. Not cock.

Piper whimpered at the sound before she saw me. Then, she came rushing to my side. I opened the back door and let her dart out. As she marked her territory, I filled up her bowls. I felt generous this morning, so I gave her two scoops instead of one, which she rejoiced over with a loud bark.

"Shh, we have a guest, and she's sleeping," I whispered.

I put my finger to my lips before petting Piper's head.

"Enjoy, Pipes. It's time for my breakfast, too, though."

I made a couple of to-go plates for people, then put the rest of the food in the fridge. I wanted to send Khloe home with food for later. But, I also promised her father and Kent a plate. Running into her father at the general store yesterday to get those donuts didn't go as roughly as expected. In fact, he'd greeted me with a smile and a hug, and even winked at me when I told him Khloe was coming over for dinner. It wasn't the anger I'd expected from him, especially after everything I had done.

Slowly, this town was starting to feel like home again.

I pulled out eggs and bacon and cheese. I arranged the donuts on a small tray and got them warming in the oven. I put on a pot of coffee and pulled out orange juice just in case. Then, I set the table for the two of us to eat. I chopped up some leftover vegetables and decided to throw all of it together in an omelet. That would go well with the donuts and the coffee.

Then, Piper started barking at the front door.

"Piper! Sh!"

But she didn't stop.

"Fuck. Piper. Cut it out. What are you doing?"

I rushed over to the front door and heard her growling, poised, and ready to attack. She kept barking, and I snapped my fingers, letting out my sharp whistle. However, when I looked out the window, I saw what she was barking at.

"Oh, shit," I murmured.

Khloe's parents were parked in front of the house, pointing at her car. I watched them talking before her mother swatted her father. I sighed heavily. Fucking hell, there was no way we'd be able to hide from them.

"I smell coffee. And bacon."

Khloe's muffled voice wafted down the stairs, and I looked up at her. She had on my T-shirt with a pair of my socks pulled up to her knees, and I couldn't take my eyes off her. She looked amazing, wearing my clothes. I felt my cock already stiffening against my pants. I took one last look outside and found her father staring at me. Through the window. Directly into my eyes.

And after he nodded at me, his mother leaned out the window to give me a thumbs-up.

Making me snort again.

"What in the world?" Khloe murmured.

I smiled out the window before turning in her direction.

"Coffee's ready, and the omelets are already on their plates. I just have to pull the donuts out," I said.

"I thought I smelled my father's donuts."

"Uh-huh. Ran by the general store at the last minute yesterday and picked them up. Figured they'd go well with breakfast this morning."

She giggled. "So, you planned on us having breakfast."

"No, actually. I wasn't planning on sharing."

"So, what are you looking at?"

I followed her into the kitchen. "What?"

"Out the window? Who was out there?"

"Uh... just—just some neighbors."

"It's my parents, isn't it?"

I watched her pour a mug of coffee before she turned

around.

"Yes," I said.

"They saw my car, didn't they?" she asked.

"Oh, yeah."

She nodded. "I figured as much. It's not like I did much to hide it."

"Did you want to hide it?"

"I mean, even if I wanted it, they live four houses up the road."

"That didn't answer my question, though."

She sipped her coffee as I held my breath.

"I don't think so," she said.

And fucking hell, I'd take it.

"You got any plans for today?" Khloe asked.

I got myself a mug of coffee before ushering us both to the table.

"Well, I do have a few errands to run. And I really need to drive down to the VA and sign some paperwork before Monday," I said.

"What's Monday?" she asked.

"My first appointment with my new therapist."

"That's good. That's really good. What time Monday?"

"Seven."

"How far away is the hospital?"

"Just under an hour and a half?"

"Holy shit, that's a serious drive."

I shrugged. "It'll be fine. And it's necessary. I still have some things I need to work through. And I promised my therapist back in Vegas, Dr. Tomb, that I'd find someone here to keep working with me."

She smiled softly. "Well, if you ever need someone to talk to in between appointments, I'm here for you."

I felt comforted by her words. "Thank you. I really appreciate that."

CHAPTER 19

KHLOE

"When was the last time this happened?" Quinn asked. "Four months ago. I figured we'd get another day off before then. But apparently not," Mom said.

I smiled. "I'm just glad we all get to go out. This never happens. It's nice."

Mom sighed. "Finally, a Sunday off! You think your father would give me more of those since Sundays are the only day Quinn takes off from the hospital."

"Hey, I didn't take off. This is just how my schedule landed," she said.

"Oh, yeah. Because you're practically attached to that place," I said.

"Maybe now that you're with Kent, you'll take more days off," Mom said, grinning.

Quinn playfully slapped Mom from the back seat, and I started laughing. When the three of us had the same day off, we always made plans to go a couple of towns over and do some shopping. Get some lunch. Millerton had the cutest boutiques and thrift shops. And then, we always got lunch by the lake at our favorite seafood restaurant.

"So, how are things with Kent?" Mom asked.

I turned around. "Yeah, Quinn. How are things now that you've locked him down?"

She shot me a look. "They're going just fine, thank you very much. We got together for some dinner last night."

"A Saturday night dinner. Classy. Where did he take you?" Mom asked.

Quinn smiled brightly. "To my favorite pizza place."

"You never were much for romance," I said.

"Hey, that place has great desserts. And he didn't even make me split one. Mine, I tell you. Desserts are all mine," Quinn said.

Mom laughed. "Well, I'm glad things are going well. He's treating you like a gentleman?"

I shot Quinn a look and silently told her to lie. She winked at me before mouthing, "Tell you later." Then, she nodded.

"Oh, yes. He's the perfect gentleman. He's wonderful, Mom."

Which, in Quinn speak, was "he's a damn animal, and I love it."

Way to go, Kent.

As we traveled through Salisbury, I tried to come up with a way to tell Quinn about Jay and me. I mean, Mom and Dad already knew. Mom had been smiling at me and winking the entire ride into Millerton this morning. And if Quinn saw any of those interactions, she'd be pissed. The town would be gossiping about it soon enough. So, I needed her to hear it from me.

Especially with Mom grinning at me like a maniac.

"So, I actually have some news of my own," I said.

"Oh?" Mom asked.

I shot her a look before Quinn slid to the front.

"What's the news? Huh? You get up to anything good this weekend?" she asked.

"Are you even buckled in?" I asked.

"I have it stretched out as far as it will go. That's safe, right?"

I snickered. "You're insane, you know that?"

"Just tell her already," Mom said.

"Wait, tell me what?" Quinn asked.

"Thanks, Mom," I said flatly.

Quinn swatted me. "What aren't you telling me?"

I cocked my body to look at her before Quinn grinned.

"No," she said.

I snickered. "I haven't even said anything."

"No, you didn't!" she squealed.

"Yes, she did. She really did. All night," Mom said.

"Mom!" I shrieked.

"Holy shit, you had a date with Jasper!" Quinn yelped.

"And she stayed the night! Dad and I found her car early Saturday morning in his in the driveway. Oh, it was so cute. I wanted to get a picture of it, but your father wouldn't let me. Such a stick in the mud, that man."

"Tell me everything. Holy hell. Why did you hide this from me, you jerk?"

Quinn slapped me again, and I slapped her back. It started a fight between us that Mom had to break up with her arm as she tried to keep the car straight on the highway. But eventually, things settled down, and my sister looked at me with massive doe eyes, waiting for my story.

"I didn't hide anything from you. I just—"

Mom kept peeking at me as Quinn smiled.

"You had a good time, didn't you?" she asked.

I sighed. "It was great. I mean, he cooked this wonderful dinner. Made breakfast. It was fantastic," I said.

"As a mom, I shouldn't be condoning this. But it's about time with the two of you."

"Really. I mean, I know you loved John. We all know you loved John. But Jasper was your first love," Quinn said.

"That you never got to explore," Mom said.

"How do you feel about all this?"

I paused. "I don't know. I mean, there's a part of me that wonders if I'm betraying John."

Mom took my hand. "But you're not, honey. I know a part of you knows that."

I nodded. "Yes, a part of me does. I don't know. I just—I can't even bring myself to sort through the guest bedroom. Am I really ready to strike something up like this with Jay, of all people?"

Quinn smiled. "Nice to hear that name again."

Mom squeezed my hand. "Yeah. It was weird, hearing you call him Jasper."

I shrugged. "It was weird calling him Jay for a while."

"Did you guys talk at all?"

"Yeah, did you get to ask him any questions?"

"Or, did you guys just get to the good stuff?"

Mom snickered. "No details, please. Let's keep it PG while I'm around."

I rolled my eyes. "I wouldn't dream of doing anything else."

"Yuck," Quinn said.

The three of us had a nice laugh as we finally crossed over into Millerton.

"Is it just me, or does this drive get longer and longer?" Mom asked.

"No distractions. I want to know if Khloe got any of her answers," Quinn said.

I smiled. "I did, actually. And honestly, it was something I should've already known."

"Why did he never call you, then?" Quinn asked.

The car fell silent as I tried to find a way to tactfully say it.

"Remember when I fell into that deep depression after John died?" I asked.

"Is that what happened?" Quinn asked.

"That makes sense," Mom said.

Quinn nodded. "I'll never forget it. For a while there, I had to force you to shower, and you wouldn't eat."

"Just think of those few months. But an entire year, an eighteen-year-old boy, and an aunt who really didn't show a lot of support," I said.

"Are you kidding me?" Mom asked.

"She didn't get him any help?" Quinn asked.

I shook my head. "According to Jay, she was just as depressed. But I guess she lashed out during her depression. You know, got angry."

"That poor boy," Quinn murmured.

Mom sighed. "Well, I'm just glad the two of you are getting back on a good track."

"Do you know where things go from here?" Quinn asked.

"No. I mean, not really. We have plans to see each other soon. But nothing more concrete than that," I said.

Mom took my hand again. "I'm happy for you, sweetie."

Quinn smiled. "Me, too."

I turned around in my seat. "Now, tell me, Quinn. How good of a kisser is Kent?"

"Are you serious?" Mom asked.

Quinn groaned. "Oh, girl. I gotta tell you about some of his tricks."

"What tricks?" Mom asked.

I laughed. "It's just kissing, Mom."

"Yeah, and what tricks is he pulling on my baby girl?" Mom asked.

"Wait, wait, wait, wait. We can practically dance around

the fact that Khloe slept with Jasper Friday night. But I can't talk about how Kent kisses?" she asked.

"She slept over, Quinn. You know your sister. She didn't sleep with the man," Mom said.

The car fell silent before my sister burst out laughing.

"What?" Mom asked.

I felt myself blush as Quinn howled with laughter.

"What am I missing?" Mom asked.

I buried my face in my hands as Quinn gasped for air in the middle of her roaring.

"Wait, did you sleep with him?" Mom asked.

"PG, remember?" I asked.

"Holy shit!" Quinn squealed.

"What have I gotten myself into?" Mom murmured.

We finally arrived at our first location, but we still had to take a few seconds to compose ourselves. Quinn couldn't stop laughing, I couldn't stop blushing, and for some reason, Mom started tearing up.

"What's wrong? You okay?" I asked.

"Oh, Mom. We're big girls. We can handle ourselves with men," Quinn said.

She sniffled. "I know. I know. It's just—"

She wiped at her tears as I looked at my sister.

"Mom, what's going on?" Quinn asked.

I took Mom's hand. "Yeah, what's on your mind?"

She sighed. "I'm just so happy that my girls are happy, you know? You've both been through such hard times. So much heartache. So much pain. And it's just—so good to see you guys laughing. And blushing. And *happy*, you know?"

I felt my own eyes watering as Quinn kissed Mom on the cheek.

"We love you, Mom," she said.

"Yeah, we do," I said.

"You and Dad have always been the perfect example of a happy relationship."

"So, thank you for giving us something positive to model."

She smiled. "I love you, girls."

"We love you, too, Mom," I said.

Quinn unbuckled herself. "Now, who's ready for some shopping?"

We all hopped out of Mom's car and started into our first of several stores. We walked up and down the aisles, and I saw Quinn already picking out an outfit for her next date with Kent. Mom kept throwing all sorts of insane clothes at her, things I knew my sister would never be caught dead in. As I giggled to myself in the corner, my eyes fell onto something.

Something tucked away in the corner.

I bent down to pick it up and heard it squeak. It startled me at first until I pulled it from behind a display.

"Oh, my gosh. That must've dropped out of my bucket. Here, I'll take that from you."

I turned around, and one of the store's workers took the squeaking thing from my hand.

"What is that?" I asked.

"Oh, we tried out a line of luxury animal toys all last month. And needless to say, it really didn't do well."

I blinked. "Do you still have any?"

She shrugged. "Most of them we donated to the local animal shelters. But I might still have a few in the back. Why?"

"Could I see them?"

"Uh, sure. Yeah. I'll be right back."

As I stood there, waiting for her to come back, I kept looking over at Quinn. She came out of the dressing room and modeled a dress that looked stunning on her. Bright red, with a pair of matching heels. She had white jewelry held up to her neck and her ears, and she looked like a million bucks.

"Quinn!" I exclaimed.

She raised her head and held up the jewelry.

"What do you think?" she yelled back.

I gave her two thumbs up as Mom clapped her hands.

"Here. This is all we've got left," the woman said.

Her voice ripped my attention back to her, and my eyes dropped to the box. There were a lot of stereotypical things. Massive bones for dogs to chew on. Squeaky toys and feathers to chase around for cats. But something purple at the bottom caught my eye.

"What's this?" I asked.

"Oh, that's a heavy-duty Frisbee."

I pulled it out of the basket. "Why does it smell like bacon?"

"Because if a dog chews through the hard plastic, there's a treat waiting for them."

I paused. "Isn't the point of a heavy-duty toy to prevent the animal from chewing through it?"

"Like I said, the ideas didn't really go over well."

I nodded. "Uh-huh."

There were a couple of interactive toys and a massive bone I thought Piper might like. So, I picked out a few things for her. And since the toys were steeply discounted, I walked away with five gifts for the good golden retriever for under thirty bucks.

Oddly enough, it felt good to spoil Piper a bit.

"Ready to head to the next store?" Mom asked.

I held my back at my side. "Ready when you guys are."

"What smells like bacon?" Quinn asked.

I snickered. "Come on. Let's go."

"No, seriously. What smells like bacon?" she asked.

"I bought some toys for Piper, and one of them has bacon

inside it. Now, can we get out of here? I'm ready to go into the bookstore," I said.

"I'm right there with you," Mom said.

"Fine. But you know Mom won't let you leave that in the car, right?" Quinn asked.

"She's right. I don't need my car smelling like fake bacon."

I rolled my eyes. "I get it. Okay? Now, come on."

And as I pulled the two of them out the doors, an idea occurred to me.

I now had a reason to visit Jay once we all got home.

CHAPTER 20

JASPER

"Willem?"

I turned around. "Yes, Chief?"

"My office. Now."

I paused. "Sir, I need to—"

"Office."

I looked over at Kent, but all he did was shrug. Shit. I had to be in my car in ten minutes if I was going to make it to my appointment. And something told me the Chief was about to hold me up. I drew in a deep breath as I walked over toward his office. I slipped inside, waiting for him to turn around.

Then, he uttered those three terrible words.

"Close the door."

Piper sat beside me as I reached around. I closed the door and felt my heart leap into my throat. I'd worked on the force long enough to know shit like this wasn't ever good. Especially with the look on Chief's face.

"What's going on, sir?"

Chief turned to face me. "I went out on a large limb hiring you."

I nodded. "I understand, sir."

"A lot of people way over my head weren't too keen on hiring someone with outwardly proclaimed PTSD."

I paused. "I understand, sir."

"So, I've been trying to do what I can to prove to them I've made the right call in you. That I've put you in the best spot I can to succeed."

"It's much appreciated, sir."

"The VA in Hartford called. I'm sure you already know how overtaxed they are."

I nodded. "Yes, sir. Though, I do have appointments set up with Dr. Shuckle."

Chief leaned against his desk. "Dr. Shuckle called me with some concerns about you traveling so far to get to appointments with him."

"He called you?"

"Yes. So, I've been working with him as well as your prior therapist to find you someone closer to home. Your doctor's main concern was the long drive back after a particularly stressful session. He's concerned about your safety. And honestly, so am I."

"So, what does this mean?"

"I want you to have all the tools you need. So, Dr. Shuckle and Dr. Tomb are in the process of transferring your paperwork to a doctor about ten minutes outside of town. Dr. Raley."

I nodded. "Thank you for all you've done, sir. I won't let you down."

"I know you won't. I know you're serious about getting help. And in lieu of you not having an appointment tonight like you thought, Dr. Tomb has made herself available for a Skype session should you need it. She wanted me to forward that to you."

"Thank you. I think I might take her up on that. Is there anything else?"

Chief sighed. "Don't disappoint me. You're under a microscope right now."

I shook my head. "I don't plan on it, sir."

"All right, Willem. Dismissed."

Kent eyed me as I walked through the room. I gave him a thumbs-up, and my partner relaxed. But I was anything other than relaxed. I had to make sure I proved my chief right. I had to make sure I proved that I wasn't a hiring mistake. I didn't understand how much tension my PTSD would kick up. Hell, I figured if they hired me, then it wasn't an issue.

Apparently, it was.

I got into my car and saw I had several missed calls on my personal phone. Two from Dr. Tomb, one from the VA hospital—which I assumed was Dr. Shuckle—and one from a number I didn't recognize.

I dialed that number back first.

Dr. Raley's receptionist answered the phone, and we went through the process of setting up an appointment for me. After that was settled, I hung up the phone and quickly called Dr. Tomb back.

"So, I take it you talked with your chief?" she asked as she picked up the phone.

"I did. And before you start apologizing, thank you."

She sighed. "You're welcome, Jasper. I know that it's pretty controversial, therapists reaching out to talk to bosses and all that. In a lot of places, that's frowned upon. But Dr. Shuckle and I thought it was best to use him as a pivot to find you a doctor as soon as possible. Especially since I'm not familiar with the doctors in that area."

"It's okay. I promise. I mean, the chief seems very willing to help me, so it's not all that bad."

"Good. Very good. So, do you want to do a Skype session tonight? The offer's on the table."

The light turned green. "Actually, I think I'm okay. For now, at least."

"Well, that's good to know. Let me know if that changes tonight, though. I'll be in the office pretty late."

"Well, I'll let you know if anything changes for tonight. And thank you for everything you've done."

"You're more than welcome, Jasper. Take care of yourself."

I hung up the phone call as I pulled into the driveway. Piper hopped out and came quickly to my side, already sensing my tension. My routine had been obliterated. And while I didn't feel myself spiraling, I wasn't grounded, either. I hung on to her scruff as we walked up to the front door. I drew in a few deep breaths as she pressed against the side of my neck. I closed my eyes. I placed my free hand against the front door.

Then, I let out a groan.

"I need a shower," I murmured.

I made my way inside and went forward with the rest of my routine. I got Piper some food and water. I shed my clothes as I walked up the stairs, then shuffled into the bathroom and turned on the hot water, ready to burn the stench of the day off my skin.

Which led me into my favorite part of my evening routine.

After drying off and getting into some pajamas, I heated up some leftovers. Piper came outside with me, and I ate on the porch, one of my favorite pastimes. I gazed up at the full moon. I felt myself relax underneath its soft glow. Dinner went down with ease before we made our way back inside. And I guess I was so grounded that Piper didn't find the need to follow me upstairs.

So, I lay in bed by myself.

With thoughts of Khloe swirling through my mind.

I wish she was here.

My bed still smelled like her. I rolled over and sniffed deeply as my cock slowly began to rise. Sleeping with her in my arms was the best night of rest I'd gotten in years. And I wanted that again. With her. I didn't think we were at a spot where I could just call her and tell her to come over, though. We weren't nearly there.

Were we?

Don't fuck it up, Jasper.

No. Better to be safe than sorry.

My muscles relaxed into the bed as thoughts of her swirled in my head. The way her body moved against mine. The silky smoothness of her skin, slithering along my body. The way she bucked. The way she rolled. And when the echoes of her soft sounds filled my ears, my cock leaped with joy. I slid my hand underneath the band of my pajamas. I gripped my girth, slowly stroking as my precum slicked my dick. I closed my eyes and imagined her there. I imagined her lips wrapped around my thickness. Imagined her humming with pleasure as the warmth of her mouth enticed me.

"Oh, Khloe," I groaned.

My cock pulsed in my palm. My breathing became ragged as the memory of her invaded all my senses. My toes curled as I envisioned her kissing up my stomach, tracing her tongue along my skin, seating herself against my pelvis, and sliding up and down my dick.

"Fuck," I growled.

I stroked faster. My back arched up from the mattress. I grunted and panted, fucking my hand while I imagined her in bed with me. Moaning. Begging for more. Spraying her juices against my body as I took her in every way I wanted. Her, riding my cock off into the sunset. Her, sitting on my face while I drank her down. Her, pinned beneath me, jumping with every thrust of my hips.

"That's it. Suck a little harder. Just like that, Khloe. Oh, hell."

As my balls curled up, my dick released, coating my stomach in strands of cum made for her body, for her and her alone.

"Oh, Khloe," I whispered.

What I wouldn't have given for her to have been with me.

CHAPTER 21

KHLOE

My eyes shot open as I gasped for air. My skin tingled and my body hummed with need for him. Holy hell, my dream had been hot. The sexiest and darkest dream I'd ever had.

With Jasper at its helm.

"Holy shit," I whispered.

I inched a hand down my stomach and under my panties, all the way to my pussy lips. I dipped between my folds, feeling how slick I had become. My head fell off to the side. I shivered and shook as my fingertips massaged my swollen clit. And as the digital clock on my bedside table struck two in the morning, my toes curled.

"Jay. Jay. Yes. Fuck—me—yeah."

Even as the pleasure cascaded through my system, though, the orgasm was hollow, the pleasure not enough. It wasn't what I wanted. It wasn't what my body needed. And the orgasm only made my body beg for more.

More of him.

More of Jay.

My eyes fell to my phone. I'd never be able to fall back

asleep. Not like this. I reached for my phone as my other hand cupped my pussy. I felt my lower lips swelling at the thought.

He's asleep, Khloe.

It didn't stop me from texting him, though.

He isn't going to respond, Khloe.

It didn't stop me from sending the message, though.

He's going to think you're insane, Khloe.

I woke up thinking of you. I hope you're okay.

And as I pulled my hand out from inside my panties, my cell phone lit up.

Funny. I'm up and thinking about you, too.

I grinned as I dialed his number.

I wonder what kind of "up" he's talking about.

"Hey there," he said sleepily.

"Well, hey," I said.

"What's got you up?"

"I should be asking you that same question."

He sighed. "Oh, you know. Same old. Just a nightmare."

I shot up in bed. "Are you okay?"

"It's nothing I can't handle."

"You didn't answer my question."

I swung my legs over the edge of the bed as silence fell over the phone.

"I suppose I could be better," he said.

"Can I do anything?" I asked.

"Nah, I'm sure you're ready to go back to sleep."

"Not if you need me, no."

He paused. "If I need you?"

"Do you need me?"

"What if I want you?"

"That works just fine with me."

He paused again. "I want you, Khloe."

I stood to my feet. "I'm coming over. I'll be there in a few minutes. Want me to pick anything up on the way?"

"No. Just get over here as quickly as you can."

"Done."

I hung up the phone and reached for my robe. And after slipping into my slippers, I shuffled toward the front door. I grabbed my keys and raced to my car. I cranked it up and did everything but speed like lightning over to his place. I rolled stop signs and blew through yellow lights. I toed the line between "illegal" and "legal" just to get to his place that much quicker. I pulled into the driveway and quickly got out, not bothering to lock my doors.

And just as I stepped up onto the porch, the front door flew open.

He reached for my wrist and tugged me into him. Jay pulled me into his house and crashed his lips against mine. He swiveled me around and closed the front door with my back. His hands pressed against the cold surface, his pelvis pinning me beneath him. His grip was tighter than usual, and his body buzzed with need.

I liked it when he came undone.

Our teeth clattered together as my arms slid around his neck. He dipped down, his hands gripping my ass cheeks. He hoisted me against his body, pulling me away from the door. As he walked us upstairs, I sucked on his lower lip.

"Khloe," he growled.

He charged us into his room and kicked his bedroom door closed. But he didn't toss me to the bed. Instead, he pinned me to the wall, sucking on my tongue and nibbling on my lower lip.

"Oh, Jay," I moaned.

"That's it. Moan for me, Khloe."

"Jay."

"Yes."

"Fuck," I groaned.

"Oh, that's it."

He kissed down my neck. He raked his teeth along my pulse point. My head fell back against the wall as his body pinned me to it. I felt him slide my panties off to the side. His teeth pulled my tank top down, exposing my breasts. I didn't even hear his pants hit the floor before his cock fell against my thigh, pulsating, leaking, ready to be inside me.

"I need you inside me. Now."

He slid his cock inside me, and my body came alive. I gasped for air as he pounded me, pushing my body farther up the wall. He buried his face into my cleavage, kissing and sucking, leaving behind soft red marks. My walls squeezed him. My body shivered for him. And as my juices dripped down his girth, he pinned my wrists above my head.

"So beautiful. So perfect. Holy shit, Khloe."

I ground against him and whimpered for more. For more of Jay. For more of his body. For more of his touch. His hands tightened around my wrists. His head came up, crashing our lips together once more. I bucked against him and felt myself unraveling, approaching a precipice as my mind fell blank, and my tits puckered with delight.

Then, he pulled me away from the wall.

"What the—?"

He tossed me to the bed, and I flopped onto my stomach. As he grabbed my ankles, he pulled me to the edge of the bed and raised my hips up. I felt my juices dripping down my thighs. He cracked his hand against my ass, making my eyes widen.

"Jay," I gasped.

But anything else was cut off as he sank his dick back inside me.

"Fuck," he growled.

The sounds of skin slapping skin filled the room. His hand wrapped into my hair, and he held my head up so he could hear every single sound I made. My body jumped with his thrusts. My heart soared with emotions. Fireworks burst in my mind's eye as my walls fluttered around him. And already, I wanted to be thrown over the edge. I wanted to come for him. I wanted to pull him over with me, spiral him into the dark, endless abyss that was the pleasure he afforded me.

"Jay," I choked out.

"Come for me, Khloe. Do it. Take me with you."

"Come with me."

My body pulled taut, and my walls clamped around him. My pussy massaged him for all he had, milking his cock empty. He rutted against me. My ass cheeks jiggled as he snapped quicker and quicker, fucking me senseless as I tumbled over the edge. He released my hair. I fisted the sheets of his bed as my face fell against them. I moaned, unearthly sounds pouring from my lips, soaking into the mattress as my thighs contracted.

"Yes, Khloe. Shit!"

Then, I felt him explode.

Thread after thread of hot arousal filled my body until it dripped down my legs along with my own. He collapsed against me, tumbling us both to the bed. With his weighted body surrounding me, I felt at peace.

For the first time since losing John.

"Jay," I whispered.

He kissed my shoulder and up my neck. I turned my face just in time to capture his lips softly against my own. Tears welled in my eyes, and he nuzzled my nose before he eased himself up and pulled his cock from between my legs.

Before we both cuddled next to one another in his bed.

"Oh, Jay," I said, sniffling.

"What is it? What's wrong?" he asked.

He held me close and stroked my hair, kissing my tears as

they fell down my cheeks.

"I can't—I don't know—"

"It's okay. I'm right here," he whispered.

"I haven't been this happy in a long time," I choked out.

He held me tighter before pulling the covers over us.

"I've got you. Let it out," he murmured.

"I'm sorry," I whimpered.

"Don't you dare be sorry for something like that. Come on."

I nodded softly. "Okay."

"Good. Now, you get it out of your system. As much as you need to."

I felt so pathetic, crying against his chest. Like the weak little girl I felt I had become. But it felt wonderful to not cry alone, for once. To not fill the darkness of my bedroom with my crying, but to be in the comfort of someone's arms while doing so. Maybe crying wasn't a weakness, after all. I mean, Jay wasn't treating me any differently. If anything, he kept pulling me closer. Kissing my forehead. Coaxing me to do more of it.

"It's okay. I've got you. I'm right here," he whispered.

"We both have to be up in a few hours."

"Four, to be exact."

I sniffled hard. "Fuck. I'm so sorry."

He gripped my chin and pulled my eyes up to meet his.

"Stop. Apologizing. I'm here for you, Khloe. Like I always should have been."

I sighed. "I'm not upset with you, you know."

He kissed the tip of my nose. "I know."

"So, you need to stop being upset with yourself."

I felt him tense, and I knew I had struck a chord.

"Just stop being so angry with yourself," I whispered.

And that was the last thing I said before the two of us drifted off to sleep.

I smelled her as my eyes came open. I felt the warmth of her side of the bed as I shifted. But when I reached out for her, she was nowhere to be found.

Which woke me up quickly.

"Khloe?"

I sat up in bed and looked around. She wasn't in the bedroom. I didn't hear any water running in the bathroom. Had it all been a dream?

No. It smells like her. She was here.

Had she left me?

I looked over at her nightstand and saw her phone sitting there. Oh, no. I knew she'd never leave without that. But then where had Khloe gone?

"Pipes?" I called out.

I whistled for her as my feet hit the floor. But I didn't hear her coming up the steps. I didn't hear her panting as she rushed down the hallway.

Where's my dog?

I groaned as I got out of bed. Something didn't sit right with me. I reached for my robe and wrapped it around my shoulders as I made my way out of the bedroom. Just as I started walking downstairs, I heard my phone alarm going off. Time for me to get ready to work and get in the shower. But I couldn't do anything like that until I found Piper.

And Khloe, for that matter.

"Hello?" I called out.

The smell of coffee lured me into the kitchen. Until I saw Piper's water bowl. Specifically, the water glistening on the floor. From where she had apparently already drunk.

"There you go. Go fetch!"

Khloe's soft voice caught my ear, and I whipped my gaze up. I saw my back door hanging open softly, so I walked in that direction. I heard Khloe giggling and Piper barking. And as I silently eased the door open, I took in the most incredible sight with my own two eyes.

Khloe, crouched down, clapping for Piper to come running for her.

And here I thought she didn't like dogs.

"Come on, Piper. You can do it. There you go! Way to go, girl!"

Watching her wrap her arms around my dog sent a punch straight to my chest. It almost took my breath away, really. As my head fell off to the side, I saw Khloe snap. Piper dropped the ball, and Khloe picked it up. Then, she launched it into the backyard. She cheered Piper on as the two of them played back and forth, with a mug of coffee completely forgotten about on the patio table.

The punch to my chest happened again. Only this time, I knew why it took my breath away.

I still love this girl.

How the hell was I going to tell her that? Should I even tell her that? "Hey, I saw you playing with my dog, and I fell in love with you again"? That made me sound like a madman. And yet, it was the truth. Every time she scratched behind Piper's ear and every time she threw that ball, I fell more and more in love with her. I fell more and more in awe of her.

So, I stood there, watching the love of my life throw a ball to the savior of my life.

"Jay! Holy shit!"

Her voice pulled me from my trance, and I grinned. She had her hand over her heart, and her eyes were wide. Very wide.

"Didn't mean to scare you," I said.

"How long have you been standing there?"

I shrugged. "Long enough for both of us to be late for work."

She paused. "What time is it?"

I leaned back to take in the clock on the wall.

"Uh, almost eight twenty."

"Holy shit, we are late," she said.

She clapped her hands and called out for Piper to follow her. But I stepped in front of her. I prevented her from going into the house, and her wide eyes went from startled to frustrated.

"You said so yourself. We're going to be late," I said.

"Gotta pay the toll first."

"What toll?"

I held my arms out. "This toll."

She snickered before walking into my arms. And when I cloaked her back, I knew I'd never go back. This was what I wanted for the rest of my life. No matter how long I had to wait for it, Khloe was the woman I wanted by my side for the rest of my days.

How the fuck am I gonna tell her that, though?

"You meant to scare me, didn't you?" she murmured.

I chuckled. "I really didn't."

"You know, that laughter tells me otherwise."

I heard Piper growling playfully, and I shot a mocking glare at her.

"Traitor."

Khloe giggled. "Hey, don't get upset with her. It's not my fault that she likes me better."

"And here I thought you didn't like animals."

"Well, maybe Piper's gotten underneath my skin."

"Or, maybe you're taking your own advice."

She paused. "Huh?"

I gripped her shoulders and pushed her out so I could gaze into her eyes.

"Maybe you're letting go of some of the emotions that have been holding you back lately," I said.

She nodded slowly. "Maybe I am."

I pulled her back in for a hug and felt her arms languidly wrap around me. Her chilly fingers slowly inched up my bare back. And I didn't even care. Everything about this felt right. Having her at my side. Making love to her at two in the morning. Waking up to her throwing the ball with Piper in the backyard before we both went into work. Everything about it, I wanted. I didn't even know I wanted it, either. Until I saw it.

Until I had it. Right there. In my grasp.

Don't screw this up, Willem.

"Want to come over for dinner tonight?" I asked.

She grinned up at me. "You gonna be cooking?"

"I figured I could make us something nice, sure."

"Or we could order in and cuddle until the food gets here."

"Mmm, I like the sound of that."

She giggled. "Good. Delivery, it is."

I smiled. "Any special requests?"

"Not pizza."

"Got it. 'Not pizza,' coming up for dinner tonight."

She stood on her tiptoes and pressed her lips against mine. Which ended with us stumbling into the shower together. I covered every inch of her body in soapy suds before fucking her senseless.

"Wow. What a morning," Khloe said breathlessly.

I kissed the nape of her neck. "I need to get dressed."

"Mmm, then you should."

I ran my hands down her naked torso. "But I don't want to."

"You'll lose your job if you don't go to work."

I nibbled her shoulder. "And we wouldn't want that."

"I've already called in late since I have to go home and get dressed. So, you might want to get a move on it."

I slapped her butt playfully, and she squealed. Yet, somehow, we managed to get dressed and get out the doors by ten 'til nine. And holy fuck, did she look good in my button-front shirt.

"You can dress like that all the time, for all I care," I said.

She unlocked her car. "I'll keep that in mind."

"See you tonight, beautiful. And wear something like that."

"Oh, you mean this old thing? Yeah, I've had it forever."

Her giggle washed over me like warm rain, and it settled my soul. We parted ways, and I rushed into work, charging through the doors right at nine. Kent stood there with a Styrofoam cup of terrible lounge room coffee. But I saw him staring at me, so my eyes dropped to my shirt.

"What? Do I have food on me or something?" I asked.

He snickered. "You're grinning."

I paused. "So?"

"A lot."

"And?"

"What gives?"

I shrugged. "Usually, people grin when they're happy."

He smiled. "Uh-huh. Any reason in particular?"

But before I could answer, a call rolled through Kent's shoulder radio, beckoning us toward the cruiser.

"Come on. Gonna be a long day today. We can grab more coffee on the road," he said.

He didn't have to tell me twice. Because I always looked for an excuse to trash the lounge room coffee whenever I could.

CHAPTER 23

KHLOE

"I think I'm going to read *Goodnight Moon* again," Matt said. I shelved another book. "Didn't you read that last week?"

"Yeah, but I've had so many parents email about how their kids ranted and raved about that story. I mean, give the people what they want, right?"

I snickered. "I'm pretty sure that's a commercialization tactic to get a consumerist society to buy more things."

"Or, it could just be my way of making six-year-olds happy in a consumerist society that will eventually eat them alive."

I turned to him. "Why are we the way we are?"

He sighed. "I really don't know. But I don't hate it."

I smiled. "Neither do I."

Usually, I hated the children's story time. I'd cordon myself in my office until it was done and over with. I didn't get along well with kids. I mean, they flocked to me, but they were always sticky and loud and begging for things. It felt a little sad, though, this time. This was one of the few story times during the week where the officers didn't have the time to get down here for it. So, the library had to provide its own hire-by-the-hour security for the hour-long event.

Which meant I wouldn't get to see Jasper.

Which seemed odd, since I'd see him three hours ago at his place before we both parted ways. I missed him already, and I wasn't afraid to admit that.

To myself, at least.

I did miss him, though. It was ridiculous to admit, but it didn't make the statement any less true. I was getting greedy with his time. Greedy with his presence. I wanted more, needed more of him. Especially now that Piper had somehow grown on me.

"Well, if *Goodnight Moon*'s the way you want to go, then I'm all for it," I said.

"You should get to the front desk," Matt said.

I furrowed my brow. "Why?"

"Just do it. Go. Go. I've got this. It's only a few more books."

"I don't—what—?"

He waved his hand at me. "Go, Khloe. Seriously."

And when I turned around, I saw why.

Quinn was standing at the front desk with her fingers flying across her phone screen. I looked back over my shoulder at Matt, who proceeded to hide behind the books he was shelving. I shook my head and snickered. The man was so finicky around my sister. Well, any woman, really. Other than me, of course. Then again, he'd been pretty finicky around me, too, when I was first hired.

Huh.

"Hey there, Q. What's—?"

She pointed at me before stuffing her phone back into her purse.

"You, me, our boys, tonight. There's a band playing in

Hartford that I like. Kent got tickets. Four, on accident. Apparently," she said.

I blinked. "Well, Jay and I kind of—"

"And wear something that doesn't look so... librarian-ish."

She ran her gaze down my body, and I scoffed.

"What does that mean?" I asked.

"It means find your fun side again. Because we're going out for some fun."

"And you didn't stop to ask me if I had any plans. You just rolled over them because, what? You thought you could?"

She quirked an eyebrow. "*Did* you have plans?"

"And if I did?"

She grinned. "You did have plans! What? What were they? With Jay? Holy shit, you had plans with Jay."

I shrugged. "Doesn't matter now. When and where are we meeting?"

"Oh, no, no, no. You're not getting off the hook that easily."

"Text me the details."

She groaned. "You suck."

"Love you, too, Q."

Quinn left on the tailwinds of the same tornado that blew her into the library. And as Matt came up to me, he made a statement that shocked the hell out of me.

And yet made so much damn sense.

"You need me to pull a Queer Eye magic trick?"

I slowly looked over at him. "A what?"

He grinned. "You know, where I take you from drab to fab?"

I turned to face him. "I knew it."

He blinked. "Knew what?"

I shook my head. "Nothing. Nothing. Uh, no. I don't need

any sort of magic trick. I'm not that far out of my twenties. I still have club clothes that fit me fine."

He smiled. "Good. Just make sure you're not trying to intentionally look sixteen again. There's a difference between looking trashy and looking classy while still going out on the town."

"You're amazing, you know that?"

"And on that note, I need to go get ready for story time."

I shook my head as he scurried off. Matthew. Gay. The sweet, innocent children's librarian who cooped himself up in the same way I did. It made so much sense. Not that it was a bad thing. It was just nice to finally have that out in the open.

Now, for the rest of my day.

I was still a bit miffed that I wouldn't get alone time with Jay tonight like I wanted. But I was still excited about the night's activities. The day flew by, and I raced home, already planning my outfit in my mind. I had the perfect top and the perfect pair of jeans. Heels, too. Not boots, though. I knew Quinn would go with boots and some skimpy skirt she had stuffed in the back of her bursting closet.

"Maybe some jewelry, too," I murmured to myself.

I skidded to a stop in front of my home and ran inside. I took a quick shower, trying to change over from librarian to hip woman out on the town for the night. I dried myself off and took the liberty of blow-drying my hair before curling it with a curling iron. It had been years since I'd done my hair up like this and splashed on this kind of makeup and pulled on jeans that were so tight they might as well have been part of me.

It felt nice, though, getting all dolled up like this.

I hadn't been a huge partier as a college girl. Or, ever. But I had a few things. I pulled my jeans up before slipping into my open-toed black heels. I reached for a white tank-top and put on my only push-up bra to really accentuate my curves. Then, I finished it all off with a black overcoat, one that cinched at my waist and flared out just above my hips. Peplum, I think it was called.

Either way, it was just the right amount of sex and class, all wrapped up into one.

The dinging of my phone caught my ear, and I reached for it. I looked down as Jasper's text and saw he was only ten minutes out. Thank fuck I got ready as quickly as I did. I rushed to put on some jewelry, though, a necklace that hung down perfectly into my cleavage, and studded earrings that glistened in the light. I fluffed my hair out, letting the wild curls grow as they wanted.

Then, a knock came at my door.

"Showtime," I said to myself.

And the way Jay's jaw dropped when I opened the door made all the rushing around worth it.

CHAPTER 24

JASPER

"Holy hell, Khloe."

She gave me a playful turn as my eyes ran up and down her curves, beautifully clad in tight clothes that left so much to the imagination it spun my head.

And made me partially upset we'd be surrounded by people all night.

"So, how do I look?" she asked.

I had to scrape my jaw off the ground. "You look… spectacular."

Like every teenage boy's dirty fantasy.

I mean, the jeans were damn near indecent. They hugged her ass so tightly I saw the outline of her ass cheeks! And her tank top. Holy shit. White, and almost see-through. Her tits were pushed up into beautiful, wondrous mounds I wanted to lick. Her heels flexed her curves even further, giving me dips and valleys my hands wanted to sink into.

It was ridiculous how quickly my cock rose for her.

"See something you like, soldier?"

I looked down quickly before I blushed. I turned my back to her and shoved my hand down into my pants. There was no hiding it now. As she giggled behind me, I made a comedic show of situating myself. Go big or go home, right? Then, I turned to face her, watching as she stepped out of her house, standing so close to me I smelled the mint of her chewing gum before she turned around to lock her damn front door.

Which pushed her ass against my groin.

"Oh, now you're just asking for it," I murmured.

"Mmm, asking for what, handsome?"

She practically purred it, and something inside me popped. It took every ounce of strength I had not to throw her over my shoulder and march her right back inside. But I did grip her hips. I did turn her around. I did pull her close, wrapping her up in my arms before letting my lips fall against hers.

The moan that fell down the back of my throat made my heart soar. I pulled those delectable curves against my body, feeling her against me. She fit me perfectly, as if I had been made for her. Our tongues did battle, and my cock ached against my pants, crying out in angry glory to be set free. Damn it, I felt myself leaking against my fucking boxers. I felt like a teenage boy again, kissing his first crush.

Hell, I was still kissing my first crush.

Kissing the first girl I ever loved.

"Mmm, heavenly," I murmured.

Khloe giggled. "You don't look so bad yourself."

"Don't even play. I don't look nearly as good as you do."

"Oh, no, no. You don't. But that doesn't mean you don't look amazing."

I snickered. "Nice save."

She smiled. "I thought so, too."

I captured her lips one last time before scooping her up. I carried her over to my truck before I sat her on the hood of it. My lips fell against her neck, and she gasped. Her head fell back, teasing the knuckles of my hands with the curls of her hair. I slid my teeth softly down to her breasts, kissing those mounds, nibbling them softly, watching as buds pressed against the white cloth of her tank top, showcasing to me just how much she wanted me.

"Jay," she whispered.

"Mmm, Khloe."

She fisted my hair and ripped me up, her eyes blown wide with desperation and need.

"Exactly how pissed is Q going to be if we skip out to use an entire box of condoms?" I asked.

Her eyes widened before she let out the most bombastic laughter I'd ever heard from her. I smiled and laughed along with her as her forehead fell to my shoulder. I wrapped my arms around her and held her close, simply enjoying the moment with her.

"Oh, Jay. I was so angry with her when she announced that she was ruining our plans tonight."

I snickered. "I'm glad I wasn't the only one."

Her head rose up. "But we gave our word we'd go. And this is Q's favorite band."

I sighed playfully. "I know. I know. Gosh."

She kissed the tip of my nose. "But if you're good tonight, maybe you'll get a nice surprise after."

"Oh, and do I get a little teaser as to what the surprise might be?"

She quirked an eyebrow before she leaned toward me, her lips only millimeters away from mine. I felt her breath against my own. My eyes closed, readying myself for another kiss. But when I felt her hand cup my raging erection, my eyes flew open.

Wide.

"This the type of teaser you're wanting?" she asked.

"Oh, you little minx," I growled.

I went to kiss her again, but she backed away. I fisted her hips and pulled her closer. But all she did was giggle and continue to lean back. She leaned back so far that she settled herself against the hood of my truck, where I proceeded to pin her wrists above her head.

"Looks like you're trapped now," I said.

"I guess the question is, do you want to be a good boy and get your surprise later? Or, do you want to be a bad boy and get nothing now?"

"I love it when you take charge."

She smiled. "Good boy. Now, let's get on the road. We're already running behind as it is."

"And I wonder whose fault is that?"

She leaned up. "Not my fault you can't stop staring."

I helped her off the hood of my truck. "Not my fault you chose an outfit that makes me want to stare."

She scoffed at me, and I winked at her. And for the first time in a while, it felt like old times. New times, too. But the playful banter was finally back. I walked around and opened her car door for her, then offered my hand. I wanted to be the perfect gentleman like my mother taught me to be. I wanted to treat her to a nice night out, especially since it seemed like she hadn't had one in a while. The drive was torment, though.

Especially with her hand sliding up and down my thigh the entire fucking time.

"That's really distracting, you know," I said.

"Good," she said, giggling.

"You're gonna be the death of me."

"If we could all be so lucky."

I grinned. "You're just full of it tonight, aren't you?"

She shrugged. "Or maybe I feel like my old self again."

I settled my hand on top of hers and looked over at her. She looked vibrant in the flashing lights over the club's rooftop atmosphere. I eased us into a parking lot and sat there, simply staring at her, drawing in her stunning features and committing all of it to memory.

"Haven't had your fill yet, handsome?" Khloe asked.

"Holy shit. Khloe. Is that you?"

Kent's voice pierced our moment before someone started knocking at my window. I looked over to see Quinn, and she smiled with delight. She ripped my door open before pulling me out of the truck. And by Khloe's squeak, Kent had done the same.

"I mean, I knew you cleaned up, Khloe. But wow. You look stunning," Kent said.

I quirked an eyebrow at Q. "Since when do you wear backless shirts?"

She gave me a small twirl. "You like? I pulled it out of the back of my closet."

"Uh-huh. And how short is that skirt?" I asked.

"Short enough for me to like the view," Kent said.

"Hey now, that's my sister," Khloe said.

I heard Kent grunt as I turned around.

"Yeah, the sister you set him up with," I said.

"Can't get pissed at me now," Kent said, grinning.

"Come on, we're going to be late. The show starts in a few minutes," Q said.

I reached out for Khlo as Q dragged us all across the street. My eyes scanned for all the exits, and Kent ended up taking a nice walk around the inside of the club once we got inside. I made a mental note of where they all were. How to get to them as quickly as possible. The best flow patterns possible in case an emergency popped up.

And the more crowded the club became, the more thankful I was that I decided to holster my gun to my hip tonight.

"You carrying?" Kent asked.

I waved at Khlo and Q, who insisted on getting the first round of drinks.

"Yep, you?" I asked.

"Yep. Good to know. There's a rooftop exit as well."

"Two fire escape ladders down either side."

"They're going to pack this place over its maximum, aren't they?"

I looked around. "Unfortunately, I think they are."

Khlo shoved a drink in my hand. "All right, you two. Cut it out."

Q stood by Kent. "What?"

She rolled her eyes. "The boys are already putting on their work faces."

Q wrinkled her nose. "What work faces?"

I wrapped my arm around Khlo's waist. "Just wanting to keep you girls safe. That's all."

Kent smiled. "Yep. We're sworn to protect, no matter what."

Q batted her eyelashes. "Oh, my hero."

I looked over at Khlo, expecting the same sort of reaction. But all she did was shrug before taking a sip of her drink.

"What?" she asked.

Kent whistled lowly. "Damn. That burns."

Khlo furrowed her brow. "Wait, what did I miss?"

I snickered playfully. "So, Kent is the big bad hero, and I'm just some schmuck on your arm?"

She shrugged. "I mean, you're a very handsome schmuck."

Q laughed. "Khloe!"

"What?"

Kent threw his head back with laughter as I pulled Khlo in to give her forehead a kiss.

"I'm just messing with you," I murmured.

"I like messing with you again."

The words were so soft, I almost didn't catch them. But

my ears didn't let me down. I gazed down into her stare, drinking in her beauty, yet again committing the moment to memory. Her eyes took my breath away. Her warmth kept me cloaked from the harshness of this world. For all I had lost in my life, I was beginning to gain hope that I hadn't lost Khloe.

That I hadn't lost everything that ever meant something to me.

"How are we doing tonight?"

The band struck a chord, and lights flashed amongst the crowd. I heard Q screaming and Kent whistling. Khlo smiled brightly as she turned toward the stage. But for me? I started searching around for Piper.

Shit. No, no, no.

"I said, how are we doing tonight?"

Another loud chord was struck, and the flashing lights started disorienting me.

Fuck. I need Piper. Where's Piper?

My eyes flickered around toward the exits. As the crowd pushed us inward, forcing us toward the stage, the sounds wrapped around me, blurring the boundary between past and present. Images flashed against the backs of my eyes. Blood. And tears. Men, crying on the side of the road.

"One more time for me. How. Are. We. Doing?"

And when that dumbass struck another loud chord, I reached for my gun.

"With me. Now," Kent murmured.

Then, I felt myself being pulled away from the girls as Kent dragged me off to the side. Away from the crowd. Away from Khloe.

CHAPTER 25

KHLOE

I leaned back to settle into Jay's body but stumbled instead. I turned around, trying to figure out where in the world he went. But Jay was nowhere to be found. My eyes scanned the crowd. I searched for Kent to try and figure out where in the world he'd gone. Quinn was jumping up and down to the music, screaming at the top of her lungs and completely oblivious to the fact that the guys weren't with us.

And when I found them, their body language was all wrong.

Kent had his hands on Jay's shoulders. Jay was practically bent over at his waist. He kept wiping at his face. His eyes kept darting around. And I knew exactly what was happening. We had to get out of here. This was too much for Jay. Way too much for him to take in.

"Quinn!"

"Woo-hoo!"

I turned around and grabbed her arm.

"Quinn!"

She faced me. "What?"

"We have to leave. Now."

She furrowed her brow but didn't question me. All she did was nod her head before her own eyes started darting around. I knew she was looking for the guys. I pulled her out of the crowd and over to the side where Kent already had Jay poised toward the exit.

"What's going on? What's wrong?" Quinn asked.

"Just hush and follow me. Come on," I said.

I prayed she didn't ask any more questions. I followed Kent on his heels as he led Jay out through a side exit. It dumped us into a side alley, where Jay's back fell against the brick wall of the club. And as Kent held his shoulders, Jay sank to his knees.

"Move. I've got him. Hold on," I said.

"What's going on? Is he okay?" Quinn asked.

"Come here. Give them space. It's okay," Kent murmured.

"Jay, can you hear me?"

His lower lip quivered. I felt his entire body shaking. His shoulders were collapsed, and his entire body looked as if it were trying to cave in on itself. I slid my hands over his shoulders. Down his back. Along his neck. Massaging his muscles and trying to relieve some of the tension so he could get himself upright. He had to get upright so he could breathe better.

I knew that all too well.

"Come on, handsome. Work with me. Listen to my voice. Lock onto my voice," I said softly.

Damn it, I wish Piper was here.

I ran my hands down his arms. I squeezed his muscles and slowly pushed him upright. I pinned his shoulders to the brick wall, watching as he struggled to catch his breath. Jay's eyes filled with tears. It sounded like he was in physical pain. I scooted closer to him. I practically straddled him. And as I continued massaging any muscle my hands fell against, I brushed my nose against his neck.

"Come on. It's just me," I whispered.

I nuzzled up and down his neck. I felt how rapid his heart rate had become, fluttering at high speed as if it couldn't gain control of itself. But slowly, Jay's heart rate settled back to normal. Slowly, his muscles unclenched. The more I nuzzled him, the more he seemed to root himself back in reality.

"There you are. Hey there. It's okay. You're with me. You're safe. You're here with me, Kent, and Quinn. It's just a concert, okay?"

"You guys okay?"

A deep voice pulled me from my soothing state and widened my eyes. I whipped my head over to see Kent stepping in between me and a massive brute of a man approaching us.

"You can't be back here. Have the four of you checked in yet?" the man asked.

"I'm a police officer over in Canaan. Everything's all right. Just got a veteran here who got a little overwhelmed in the club."

"Make him go away," Jay breathed.

I looked over at the man. "I promise we'll leave once I can get him up. He just needs some time."

The man's eyes searched us before he nodded.

"You guys need me to call anyone?" the man asked.

Holy fuck, go away. "No. Thank you. I appreciate the offer, though."

"Make him go away," Jay wheezed.

I went back to rubbing Jay's chest. I nuzzled his neck, massaged his shoulders, and ran my hands down his back. I had to get him settled. I had to get him to come down off this emotional high he was running on. And as the bouncer's footsteps finally backtracked, Jay's hands fell against my hips.

Squeezing as tightly as he could.

"I'm sorry," he choked out.

"Hush. None of that nonsense right now. Conserve your energy, all right?" I asked.

"I ruined the—"

I shook my head quickly. "You ruined nothing."

Quinn piped up. "She's right. You're good. Everything's fine, okay?"

I placed my lips against Jay's ear as I massaged his arms.

"Just focus on my voice. Nothing else. Focus on the sound. The breath falling from my lips. Focus on how good it will feel to get back in your truck and head to my house. Where it's nice and quiet. The wind whipping through the trees. Me, getting a pot of coffee ready. Sharing some cinnamon rolls from the oven. Would you like that?"

He drew in a shuddered breath. "Yeah. Yeah, I would."

"All right. Then, focus on your breathing. And when you can stand, we can get out of here. Okay?" I asked.

It felt like an eternity before Jay finally grounded himself. But when he did, he wrapped his arms tightly around me. He buried his face into my neck and breathed in deeply, almost as if he were sniffing me. I hugged him tightly. Kent helped the two of us up before Jay disconnected from me. And as his hands cupped my cheeks, I reached for his pocket to dig around for his keys.

"Ready to go?" I asked.

Jay offered a weak smile. "You just wanted to get into my pants, huh?"

I giggled. "Maybe a little bit. Can you really blame me, though?"

His eyes danced around my face. "Not one bit."

"Here, let me help you to the truck. I'm sure Khloe here won't have an issue driving back," Kent said.

"And don't you even think about fighting. We need to make sure you get somewhere safely," Quinn said.

We all walked with Jay back to his truck. After Kent helped him into the passenger's seat, I hugged Quinn tightly.

"I'm so sorry about tonight," I whispered.

She kissed my cheek. "Shut up. Don't even apologize. Just call me when you're home safe. Wherever you two end up at. Okay?"

I nodded. "Okay. I promise."

"Good."

Kent settled his hand on my shoulder. "You take care of him tonight, all right? No caffeine, don't pump him full of sugar, and get him to take a hot shower before he goes to bed tonight."

I nodded. "Done, done, and done. I told Quinn I'd call her once we were safe."

He pulled me in for a hug. "Keep yourself safe, too."

I hugged him tightly, then waved goodbye to them. Quinn tugged Kent back to the club as I wrapped around and climbed into the driver's seat of Jay's truck. He leaned against the window, drawing in deep breaths. And as I struck up his truck, I felt something warm against my knee.

Jay's hand.

Which made me smile when I gazed down at it.

"I'm going to take you back to your place. I think you'll be more comfortable there. Okay?" I asked.

But all he did was grunt.

The drive back to his place was fast and quiet. I hit all the green lights at all the best possible times, and it cut our travel time almost in half. By the time we pulled into the driveway, we hadn't been traveling for more than fifteen minutes or so.

Then, he broke.

"I'm sorry. Holy shit, I'm so sorry, Khlo."

I parked the truck. "I promise it's okay. Jay, listen to m—"

"I'm sorry. I'm sorry. I ruined the night. I couldn't keep it together. I'm so sorry."

"Jay, look at me."

"I'm so sorry," he whimpered.

I unbuckled myself and jumped out of the truck. I rushed over to the front door and fiddled with the keys as I heard him crying in the truck. The sound broke my heart. Tears dripped down my cheeks as my hands shook.

"Come on!" I exclaimed.

Then, I finally slid the house key into the damn lock.

"Piper! Come here, girl! Piper, sweetie!"

A resounding bark wafted down the hallway before she rushed past me. I heard her growling, already sensing Jay's unhinged state. I wiped away my tears as I ran back to the car, opening Jay's passenger door. I helped him to the ground, right beside Piper, where he clung to her fur and kept apologizing over and over again.

As if he had done something wrong.

"I'm so sorry. Please, forgive me. Holy fuck, I'm so sorry. I'm sorry, you guys. I'm sorry."

And as I knelt beside him, rubbing his back, I pulled my cell phone out of my pocket.

Hey, Quinn. We made it back to his place. Getting him inside now. You two have fun tonight. Tell me all about it tomorrow. Love you.

Now, if I could only get Jay into his house.

CHAPTER 26

JASPER

The first thing I felt was the existential pain in my head. Like someone had drilled a hole straight through the top. I grimaced as I licked my lips. And the nasty taste in my mouth grated against the chapped skin of my lips. I couldn't breathe through my nose. It felt almost impossible to open my eyes. I turned my head, wincing as I did so. Because the electric pain shooting down my neck pierced straight to my gut.

Why does it hurt to be awake?

As my eyes slowly fell open, I wished they hadn't. The morning sun was blinding, making my headache worse. My eyes felt sore. It was hard to keep them open. I hadn't ever felt like this before. Even after a panic attack, I usually shook it off with a—

Holy shit.

The panic attack.

"Khloe?" I groaned.

"Mhm?"

I was shocked to hear her voice, especially with how bright it was outside.

"You're here?" I asked.

She laughed softly. "Where the hell else would I be?"

"I don't know. Work."

"I mean, I could technically say the same thing about you. But here we are."

I winced as I moved my head. I lobbed it over toward the direction of her voice and found her sitting in a chair on my side of the bed. She had her leg crossed over her knee, and her tangled hair tossed over one of her shoulders. My button-down shirt fell off her shoulder, and those tight-as-hell jeans made me lick my lips.

"Here, drink this."

My eyes focused on a bottle coming at me. Something orange. Something bright. And when the word Gatorade came into view, I considered proposing to her then and there.

"Come here, I'll help you sit up," she said.

"You don't have t—"

"You wanna try on your own? Because I don't think you're going to get very far with that."

I paused. "Why do I hurt so badly?"

"Drink, then we talk."

Her arm slid under my back, and she hoisted me against the headboard. I groaned as my muscles screamed out in pain. She guided the drink to my lips and softly tilted it up, giving me enough time to swallow before tipping it up even further. I let my eyes fall closed. I drank down the glorious liquid as if it were my life's force. After a few deep gulps, she placed the drink down before dabbing my shirt she was wearing against the dribbles on my chin.

"I called Matt when I first woke up. Told him I needed a sick day. So, you're kind of stuck with me," Khloe said.

"I could never be merely stuck with you, Khlo."

She kissed my cheek. "Let's get you showered. Then, we should talk about some stuff. Okay?"

I furrowed my brow. "Something tells me you don't want to talk about the panic attack last night."

"Shower first. I couldn't get you into one last night. So, you probably stiffened up a lot while you were asleep."

"Khlo, is everything—"

She gazed into my eyes. "Hot shower. Now. Come on."

She helped me out of bed and led me to the bathroom. I took the quickest shower of my entire life. If this talk was about us, then I wanted it to be over quickly. I wanted to get it out of the way and deal with the heartache that ultimately came with all of these kinds of conversations. I mean, on the one hand, I didn't think Khloe to be the kind of girl to stop seeing someone based on something like this. She was much too good of a person.

On the other hand, though? We hadn't even talked about what we were doing. So, maybe all of this was too much for her.

Maybe I had come on too strong.

I let the hot water batter against my muscles before I washed my hair. I dried off at lightning speed, and with every movement, I felt the stiffness falling away from my body. Not knowing what she wanted to talk about was killing me. I threw on the first items of clothing my hands pulled out of my drawers before charging down the stairs. She had left my room completely, and I didn't know where she had gone.

Until the smell of coffee hit my nostrils.

"Khlo?"

She didn't answer, so I followed the smell. I didn't find her in the kitchen, though. I walked into the living room. I made my way into the dining room. I even checked back upstairs.

I found her on the porch with two mugs of coffee sitting on the glass table.

"Have a seat," she said.

I sat down and braced myself for what was coming. I picked up my coffee and took a long pull of it. I heard Piper bark, and it made me jump, sloshing coffee all over my lap.

"Come here, girl. There you go. Come on, drop it. Drop it. Piper. Drop. Now."

I snickered as Pipes finally dropped the ball. Then, Khloe reached for it. She cocked her hand back and threw it far, much farther than my eyes could track the ball. Impressive, to say the least. And as Piper scurried away after it, Khloe settled back into her seat.

"I wrote out a list on my phone, so I wouldn't forget all the things I want to talk about. But first? I want to address your apologizing."

Her voice pierced the silence between us as she turned to me.

"Jasper, I want you to hear me when I say this. Okay?"

I nodded. "I'm listening."

"I don't even know if you remember what happened last night. But when we got back to your place? You unleashed. You kept apologizing. Over and over. For something that isn't even your fault. You don't ever have to do that. Don't do that. You never need to apologize for having a panic attack. Not after what you've been through."

I nodded.

Her warm smile chased away my fears and the dread filling my gut. She set her phone down on the table as Piper barked in the distance, signaling to us that she'd found that damn ball. All of my fears dissipated as she scrolled through her phone. I sipped my coffee, waiting for her to gather her own thoughts.

And as Piper ran across my backyard, Khloe looked up at me, before taking my hand within hers.

"The first thing I want to talk about is how important Piper is to your stability," she said.

"She's a pretty big rock in that arena, yeah," I said.

"I figured that out last night. It should've occurred to me to ask you about it. But it also should've occurred to you to step up and tell me that you couldn't go anywhere like that without her."

"I guess I just didn't—think I'd struggle with it like I did. Not as badly, anyway."

She nodded. "Well, from now on? Even if you think you might possibly struggle with something? Speak up. Tell me it's not a good idea. I don't ever want to put you in another situation like that ever again. No matter who made the plans or bought the tickets or any other shit like that."

My God, you're incredible. "Got it."

"We go nowhere without Piper. And if Piper can't come? We don't go. It's as simple as that."

You're outstanding. "Deal."

"The second thing on my list: Quinn."

"Quinn?"

"Well, more specifically, people around here who were close to you when you were a child. When we were all children. I didn't think it was my place last night to tell her explicitly what was going on. But I think she figured it out."

I was lucky to have you there. "She's always been a smart girl."

Khloe squeezed my hand. "Quinn walked me through little attacks like that when I first lost John. Nothing major. Not like what you experienced. But she was there for me. She knows what the bare bones of something like this look like."

"Do you still deal with them?"

"This isn't about me right now. This is about—"

"Khloe, that question is important to me."

She kissed my hand. "And we will talk about it. After we're done talking about you. Okay?"

You're perfection. "Promise me."

She smiled. "I promise."

I mean, just look at those beautiful eyes. "Good."

"It wasn't my place last night to tell her what was going on. But I think she should know. I think you should start viewing the people around you—like me and Kent and her and my parents—as a life support raft. And rafts only function normally if they're fully inflated."

You're all I need. "With knowledge, in this particular metaphor."

"Yes. With knowledge. You can do it on your own time, in your own way. But I think it would be very beneficial for your sake if y—"

Marry me.

She blinked. "What?"

"What?"

"Did you just say 'marry me'?"

Holy fuck, did I say that out loud? "Did I?"

She licked her lips. "Yeah, I think you did."

Might as well roll with it. "Yeah, I did."

"Marry you."

"Yes, marry me."

She snickered. "You're asking me to marry you?"

Yes. "More a statement than a question, but yes. I am. Marry me."

CHAPTER 27

KHLOE

I leaned back into my chair. "What the fuck, Jasper?"

Silence fell between us as Piper rubbed her fur up and down my leg.

"You can't possibly be serious," I said.

"And what if I am?" he asked.

"Then, I'd ask you if you're suffering from some kind of episode right now."

"Why, because I love you?"

"Oh, come on."

"No, you come on. Listen to me. Khlo, I've always loved you. So, for once, instead of running away scared, I'm going to own up to how I feel."

I sighed. "I can't marry you, Jay."

He leaned forward. "Why are you still here?"

I blinked. "What?"

"Why are you here? Right now?"

"Because I stayed the night with you."

"And why did you do that?"

"Well, because I—"

He reached for my hand. "Say it, Khloe."

I placed my hand against his. "Because I wanted to make sure you were okay. I was worried about you."

"Yes. And then I woke up this morning, and instead of you being gone to work, you called off. Why?"

I shrugged. "I wanted to make sure you had someone around."

"And now, we're out here. Discussing how we can be better about this in the future. We. Us. As a cohesive unit."

"I guess we are, sure."

"So, if you don't love me back, why aren't you running away from my crazy ass? Why are you here? Trying to take care of me instead?"

I shook my head. "Did you ever think that it might possibly be too soon to even think about asking something like that?"

He nodded. "I have, yeah. It doesn't change anything, though. Marry me, Khloe."

"You're crazy, you know that?"

He grinned. "It's why I have a therapist. Marry me, Khloe."

"This can't possibly go over as well as you think it might."

"We'll never know until we try. Marry me, Khloe. My best friend. The only person who ever made me feel worth something in this world."

"I'm sure I'm not the only person, but okay."

His eyebrows rose. "Okay… what?"

I felt my heart swell with delight at the taste of that word on the tip of my tongue.

"Okay, I'll marry you," I said.

He blinked. "Are you serious?"

I snickered. "Yeah. Holy hell, I guess I'm saying yes."

He smiled at me, and I fell apart in laughter. I heard him laughing with me, the song bouncing off my ears. I felt a little hysterical. Tears rushed to my eyes. I felt apprehensive.

And hurt. And weirded out. But mostly happy. Very happy, really.

And definitely *not* scared.

"Jasper," I said breathlessly.

He scooted his chair closer to me. "I love you, Khloe."

My gaze met his, and his smile broadened.

"You don't have to say it. Not until you're ready. But I need you to look in my eyes and know it's the truth. I've always loved you. I never stopped loving you. No matter where life took us, and no matter what your life became, I knew I'd always love you. First, as a friend. And second, as the only girl I've ever loved."

I cupped his cheek. "Oh, Jay."

He cupped the back of my hand and kissed my palm. And as my heart leaped into my throat, I felt myself spiraling. This was all too fast. Too impulsive. Too much. But I did love him. Greatly. And considering the experience I had in my life with men I fell in love with, I didn't want him to get away. Not again. Not without being able to express to him how much he meant to me.

How much he'd always mean to me.

"Kiss me," I said softly.

His eyes came back to mine before he tugged me to my feet.

"Kiss me and don't let go," I breathed.

He pulled me into him, wrapping his arm around my waist. And as his lips came down against mine, Piper let out a resounding bark. I wrapped my arms around his neck, holding him close. I jumped, locking my legs around him as he carried me back inside. I sucked on his lower lip and ran my fingers through his hair. I couldn't get enough of him as he walked us up the stairs.

I broke away from the kiss long enough to lean over his shoulder, to look behind him, and snap my fingers.

"Piper, stay."

She whimpered but did as she was told.

"Good girl," I said with a grin.

"You're my good girl," Jay growled.

He pinned me to the wall and ripped my shirt over my head. My bra came off in a frenzy as his hands massaged my tits. My nipples puckered as I felt his tongue lingering against my peaks. I moaned for him and gripped his hair, pushed him farther into my cleavage as his growls shook my rib cage. My heart soared for this man. My body heated with a need for his presence. And as his teeth marked my tits, making them his once and for all, I choked out my next words.

"Shower. Hot. Now."

He peeled me away from the wall. He walked us into the bathroom. He set me on the bathroom counter before kissing down my neck, giving him time to slide the rest of my clothes off. I was naked for him, bare, dripping, and ready for his taking. His eyes scanned me with a carnal lust I wanted to indulge. Then, he turned around and fiddled with the shower before stripping down in front of my eyes.

I licked my lips as his muscles came into view. I noticed a couple of tattoos I hadn't seen yet. I couldn't make out what they were, but I didn't really care. All I wanted was to feel his body against mine.

"Come back to me," I said.

I held my arms out for him, and he rushed toward me.

"I'll always come back to you, Khlo."

I captured his lips in a sizzling kiss. We stumbled into the hot shower as water beat against our skin. I felt him everywhere, his cock pulsing against my thigh as he held me, pinned to the wall. Water dripped over the divots of his muscles. I felt his lips slinking down my skin, lower and lower, until he set me down on my feet and tossed my leg over his shoulder.

"Let me taste you," he groaned.

I gripped his hair as his tongue pierced my folds, licking me, stroking me, sucking on my swollen clit until my thighs shivered with a need for release. I bucked ravenously against his face. I felt myself come alive. I felt my body tense. And as his tongue buried itself in my entrance, my body locked up.

"Jasper!" I wailed.

Juices sprayed from between my legs. My entire body went weak as my orgasm crashed over my senses. My nipples tightened so much it hurt. My nails raked over Jay's scalp, and I lost all sense of time and space as pleasure washed through my system, factory resetting me as my legs finally gave out.

"I gotcha. I gotcha. Come here, beautiful."

He lowered me to the shower floor and hovered his beautiful body over mine. With his smiling face and those beautiful eyes looking down at me, I felt my heart skip a beat. Water poured over his edges, framing him as if he were a natural waterfall.

"Kiss me," I whispered.

"You'll never have to tell me twice," he murmured.

Softly, his lips brushed mine, leaving me with a need to taste myself against his skin. I clapped my hand around the back of his head, pulling him down to me, forcing his muscles to fall against my curves. I spread my legs wide for him until his cock was seated at my entrance. And as I relaxed underneath him, his cock filled my body, sliding against my throbbing walls.

"Khloe," he grunted.

He snapped his hips against mine, over and over, as hot water battered against our bodies. I couldn't get enough of him. The way he moved against me. The way our bodies fit one another like a glove. The electricity he afforded me and the way he pushed me to wondrous heights. I raked my teeth down his neck. I heard him grunting as I nibbled on his shoulder. With my nails marking his back, he pounded into me, faster and faster, as his dick thickened against my walls.

"That's it. Don't stop. Holy shit, Jay."

"I'll never stop. Never, Khlo. I love you. I love you. I love you."

The sounds of wet skin slapping wet skin filled his walk-in shower. His movements grew ragged as his breathing picked up. I hung on for dear life, my body jumping against his.

"Jay, please!" I wailed.

"Come for me, Khlo. Do it," he growled.

"Oh, shit."

"Yes. Yes. Yes. Squeeze that—fuck!"

My walls clamped down around him, and he fell over the edge with me. Bursts of hot arousal coated my walls with every flutter of my body. I pulled him deeper, milking his cock for all it had

"That's it. That's it. Oh, Jasper. Oh, shit. Oh, my god."

"Mine," he grunted.

He collapsed against me, pinning me to the shower floor as the scalding water washed away the evidence of our debauchery. I nuzzled the side of his face and kissed the shell of his ear. I felt his cock filling me, still seated between my legs as if it had found its home.

As if Jasper had found *his* home.

With me.

I kissed his shoulder. "We should maybe not tell anyone yet."

Jay stiffened. "Why do you say that?"

"Sh, it's okay. Nothing bad. Relax. I just think we should

sit on this until we're both not feeling quite so... raw from it all."

He nodded slowly. "That makes sense."

"And, you know, until we've been seeing one another maybe longer than a month."

He chuckled. "You always knew how to make some great points."

"I suppose it's one of my many talents."

"And oh, you do have many of them."

I grinned. "I suppose I do."

With every kiss, I sighed in relief. With every movement of his body, I shivered in anticipation. I felt spent. And yet, I wanted more. I wanted it all. With him. Forever.

I love you, Jay.

"Is everything all right?"

His question pulled me from my trance, and I smiled up at him.

"Everything's perfect," I said.

And I meant every syllable of it.

CHAPTER 28

JASPER

"Willem!"

I turned around. "Yeah, Chief?"

"It's four. Get out of here."

I grinned. "Yes, sir."

"And give me a call to let me know how this first session goes."

"Will do, sir!"

I rushed out of work with Piper hot on my heels. I was thankful the chief was letting me off early today. Because I needed to do this. I needed to go to my therapist's appointment as relaxed as I could get. I didn't need to be in my uniform or still smelling like sweat from running around all day. And I needed to make sure Piper got some food and water before I took her with me.

I was thankful to have a chief that understood that.

"Come on, girl. We have some dinner to get really quickly," I said.

Piper answered me with a resounding bark.

As I made my way back to my place, I thought about this

past weekend. The days I spent lying around with Khloe, talking about all the things that had happened back in Vegas. I told her about the time I first saw Dr. Tomb. How hesitant I had been and how angry I still was inside. I didn't think anyone could understand me. I didn't think anyone could possibly understand what I was going through. I told Khloe how my doctor surprised me. How she unlocked ways for me to cope and gave me my first safe space ever since I had first arrived in Vegas as a scared seventeen-year-old little boy.

And through it all, Khloe was supportive of me going back to therapy.

Hell, I needed it, too. After a spur-of-the-moment marriage proposal and the subsequent shock that came with her actually accepting, I needed to talk with someone. Was I teetering on another ledge? Was I making a mistake? Would this blow up in my face?

I didn't want it to.

But I also wasn't an idiot.

Mostly.

It warmed my heart, how supportive Khloe was being. She even offered to come over to my place after my therapy appointment. Just to talk. Just to be here with me. I took her up on the offer, of course. I wanted her here with me. As much as I could get of her, no matter the form it took.

You didn't make a mistake, Jasper.

That didn't mean I wouldn't bring it up with my therapist, though.

After getting home and cleaning myself up, I got Piper some food. I brought a portable water bowl with me, just in case. Then, we were back on the road. With my hair clean and my body scrubbed down and my comfortable clothes already easing me into the routine, I headed for Dr. Raley's office, ready to fill out paperwork, talk the poor man's ear off, and try to find some equal footing to stand on with everything that had happened.

"Welcome to Dr. Raley's, are you checking in?"

The familiar voice made me smile. "Jasper Willem. I have an appointment at—"

"Five-thirty! Yep. I remember you. Here's the paperwork you need to fill out. Pretty standard. You and your adorable dog can take a seat anywhere you like."

I nodded. "I appreciate it."

Piper wore her vest with pride as we tucked ourselves away in a corner. The paperwork was as standard as it came —bubble sheets to fill in to determine how anxious I was in any given scenario, how hard my depression usually hit, whether or not my depression made me suicidal. I filled in the answers honestly, because really, what did I gain from lying to my new doctor? My chicken scratch covered the lines, and I hoped Dr. Raley didn't have any issues reading my handwriting.

"Mr. Willem?"

The woman's voice caught me off guard. I whipped my head up and saw an older woman standing there, with salt-and-pepper hair with thick red-framed glasses. She had on a Christmas sweater vest with a plaid skirt and shoes that looked way too comfortable and casual for a setting like work. She almost reminded me of a grandmother. A kind, comforting grandmother, knitting somewhere in a corner with sweet treats in her pocket.

And when my eyes fell to her name tag, I almost swallowed my tongue.

"Dr. Raley?"

She smiled. "You must be Jasper. Come on in."

I paused. "For some reason, I was under the impression that you were—"

"A man? Well, my husband works here, too. It gets a bit

confusing. But you're with me. Unless you'd feel more comfortable speaking with him."

"I uh, it's just—some of the things I struggle with—"

She ushered me into her office. "Why don't we talk it over? And if you would still rather speak with him after our session, I'll get you transferred seamlessly. How does that sound?"

I nodded. "I'm sure that can't hurt."

I walked back into her office and sat on the couch. Piper settled herself at my feet, watching Dr. Raley with a careful eye. She closed her office door and sat down, scanning my paperwork, flipping over sheets, and nodding her head softly as if she were taking the time to drink in all the information.

"I'm aware of your military record, Mr. Willem. And I just want to say—"

I held up my hand. "Please, don't thank me for anything."

She smiled. "I was going to say, I understand more than you realize. But I'll keep that in mind."

I blinked. "Oh."

"Why don't you like people thanking you for your service?"

"Well, because I didn't join to serve my country. I joined because I didn't have any other option."

"You could've taken out student loans to try and make it in college. Or gotten a job washing dishes somewhere."

I shrugged. "Guess the military provided a slightly better structure for me. At the time."

"So, it had nothing to do with even being slightly brave enough to sign your life away to a governmental institution that can send you into some of the worst places on this earth whenever they see the need? You know, rather than washing dishes at a diner."

I leaned back into the couch. "I don't really know."

The entire hour was spent not with me talking at her but

talking *with* her. She was unique. Vocal. Open in her opinions and willing to listen to mine. It felt as if I were speaking with an old friend than a doctor. And I liked it. I found myself talking about all sorts of things. Basic training. The first time I went back to Vegas for leave. My relationship with my aunt. And just as Dr. Raley learned things about me, I learned things about her.

Like the fact that she and her husband had met when they were *both* enlisted.

And the fact that she had a service dog, too.

And the fact that she still had to utilize ways to deal with her own PTSD flashbacks.

She was a breath of fresh air. Once the hour drew to a close, I had no issues scheduling my next four sessions with her, and her alone. I felt emotion weighing me down, making it harder to move. But Dr. Raley assured me it was normal.

"However, if it doesn't alleviate with a hot toddy and a good night's sleep, you call this office first thing in the morning. Okay?" she asked.

I nodded. "Okay. I can do that."

"Good. I'll see you in a week, then. And if I get another opening sometime in the afternoon this week, I'll give you a call. See if you want to come in."

I liked that she already knew I'd want that.

"I appreciate that. Thank you," I said.

I walked out to my truck, and Piper jumped in. The first phone call I placed was to Chief, letting him know how the appointment went. He seemed proud enough. A bit relieved, too. And after hanging up the phone with him, I sent a text to Khloe.

Heading home. The appointment went well. Can't wait to see you.

The emotional heaviness sitting against my chest slipped away the second I saw her standing there on my porch, waiting for me as I pulled into the driveway. She smiled brightly as I got out, then rushed toward me as I came around the truck. And as her arms wrapped around my neck, she crashed her lips against me, sending me hurtling toward the hood of my truck as the fury of her kiss seized my heart.

CHAPTER 29

KHLOE

I sighed as I pulled into my driveway. It made my heart *so* happy to see him in my space. To see his truck parked out in front of the house. To see his shadowed presence walking around behind the curtained windows of my quaint little cottage. But I preferred to spend time at his house. Sure, they both held sad memories. But with him being so close to my parents, it made things more comfortable in an odd sort of way.

Like, if something went wrong, they were right there as opposed to all the way out here where no one could get to us quickly.

Like no one could get to John.

I shook the thought from my head. We weren't at that point yet. Moving in together, and whatnot. Then again, we were engaged. Wasn't that what engaged people did? Move in together? Or, at least planned to move in together?

You don't even have a ring yet.

Did I need a ring to be engaged, though?

That's kind of how that works.

"No, that isn't how it works. You get engaged because you're in love. Not because of some ring," I murmured.

Do I love Jay, though?

I turned off my car and gazed through the window. I saw Jasper walking around, doing something in the living room. He bent down before he came up. And I watched him fluff something. I squinted my eyes at his movements. It was hard to make out what he was doing. But if I saw things correctly...

He's cleaning your damn house.

I smiled brightly. I unclipped my seat belt and started for my house. With each step I took, I felt my heart fill with delight. I walked through the front door and looked to my left. I saw Jay tossing the folded blanket over the couch. My place smelled of lemon and honey. The floors shined, and the carpets looked freshly vacuumed.

"What in the world are you doing?" I asked.

He grinned. "Just helping out a bit. You thirsty?"

"Are you saying my house is dirty?"

"No, I'm saying that sometimes people need help."

I giggled. "Is that why you came by the library and stole the keys to my house? Because you thought I needed help?"

"Okay, can't a man just do something nice for his woman every once in a while?"

My heart leaped at his words. "His woman?"

His gaze found mine. "Yes. His woman. *My* woman."

I do love him. "I think I like the sound of that."

He winked. "I hope so. Because you kind of agreed to marry me."

"Eh, kind of."

He chuckled. "Come in here, beautiful."

I dropped my things at the door and rushed into the room. I leaped into his arms, and he swung me around as

Piper barked up a storm. He set me down on my feet, and she jumped at my legs, wanting nothing more than to get in on the moment.

"Hey there, cutie pie. Are you helping Jay clean my house?" I asked.

Piper barked, and it made me smile brightly.

"I bet you're a big helper. Yes, you are. Yes, yes, yes, you are."

Jay chuckled. "You're adorable, you know that?"

I slid my hand down Piper's back. "Not as adorable as this little girl right here. Yes, hi there. I missed you, too, sweet girl. Mhm. Yes, I did."

"Come here, you."

Jay gripped my chin and pulled me upright, turning all of my attention to him. And when he did, his lips captured mine, and I draped my arms around his neck. I felt him groan down the back of my throat as I pressed against him, ready to bring a close to the very short week the library had this week.

"Mmm, well, hello there," I said, giggling.

"You ready for the long weekend?" Jay asked.

I nuzzled his nose. "I'm always ready for something like that. Do you have a long weekend?"

He nodded. "That, I do."

"Sounds exciting."

"It is."

"Sounds like I get to see a lot of you on this long weekend."

His hands fell to my hips. "It's supposed to snow, you know."

"Mmm, first snow of the season."

"And my house has a fireplace."

"That, it does."

"And a television."

I smiled. "A mounted television."

"With hot apple cider and warm, fluffy blankets."

I grinned. "And a very nice man to keep me company, I hear."

He winked. "Maybe not too nice, though."

I captured his lips softly. "Sounds like we're headed back to your place, then."

"Mmm, especially since your place is such a mess."

My jaw fell open. "What?"

He threw his head back, laughing. "Well, it is."

I swatted his chest, giggling. "You're disgraceful. Just disrespectful. A heartbreaker."

I pulled away from him and walked into the kitchen, ready to crack open a bottle of wine. His laughter followed me into the room, but all I did was shoo him away.

"I will never break your heart again. Not if I have anything to do with it. Do you hear me, Khlo?"

His voice snapped me out of my playful mood, and I found his gaze. So stern. So stoic. So serious. I cupped his cheeks and brought him in for one last kiss. One that lingered. One that sizzled. One that caused my nipples to pucker against my bra.

"I hear you," I whispered against his skin.

"You're everything I've ever needed in my life," he murmured.

His lips fell to my neck as Piper barked in the other room.

"You're everything I've ever dreamed of," he groaned.

His teeth nipped at my pulse point, causing me to gasp.

"Jay," I whispered.

"And I'll do anything—anything in my power—to make sure you're always happy," he breathed.

His hands gripped my ass, and he pulled me away from

the refrigerator. He picked me up, carrying me back into the living room. We tumbled to the couch. With one snap of his fingers and a whistle of his lips, Piper retreated, giving us some much-needed privacy as he sank my body against the cushions of the couch.

"I love you, Khlo. And however long it takes for us to get married, or start telling people about us, or even to start processing it ourselves, I'm willing to wait. Because you're worth it. You always were. And you always will be."

Tears crested my eyes. "Jasper."

"Yes."

His forehead fell against mine as tears trickled down the sides of my face.

"Maybe we don't need to wait," I whispered.

He kissed my lips softly. "What do you mean, beautiful?"

I sniffled. "I mean, maybe we should start telling people."

"Even before we've gone ring shopping?"

I shrugged. "Why not?"

I found his gaze and watched his brow furrow tightly.

"Jasper, getting engaged isn't about a ring. It's about love. And happiness. And—and cohesion. I love you. I love you so much, and—and telling people about us doesn't scare me. The engagement. Us being together. None of it scares me."

"Really?"

I nodded. "Really. So, whenever you're ready, I'm ready."

A soft growl fell from his lips before he sank against me. His kiss filled me with joy, and his hands filled me with fire. Our clothes came off in a flurry. Our bodies connected as one. And as we marked our place on the couch in my living room, I chanted those words effortlessly. As if my throat had broken some imaginary seal.

"I love you. I love you. Jay, yes. Please. I love you so much."

"Fucking hell, Khlo. I love you. You're perfect for me. So fucking—shit!"

We made love until we dripped in sweat. Until the couch smelled of nothing but us. Then, he collapsed on top of me, and I pulled a blanket over us. He panted into the crook of my neck. I felt our intermingled juices dripping from between my legs, further wetting the couch underneath my body. I stroked my fingertips up and down his back, feeling him jump as his lips mindlessly kissed the skin of my shoulder.

Then, he lifted his head.

"Who do you want to tell first?" he asked.

I paused. "I'm not going to lie, Quinn will be pissed if she's not the first."

He grinned before he reached down, laying his body weight on top of me. I giggled and held tightly to him as his arm sifted around. He kept reaching. Moving. Sliding. Inching closer to the edge. And when I felt both of our bodies tilting over the edge, I locked my legs around his waist.

"Jay!" I exclaimed.

We rolled off the couch and tumbled onto the floor in a fit of laughter. My body slid off to the side, covered haphazardly in the blanket. I looked up and saw Jay dicking around with his phone, pressing button after button before cradling me close.

"Smile for the camera," he said.

"Don't get my boobs in there, geez," I said breathlessly.

He chuckled. "This is going to Kent and Quinn. Trust me, no boobs for them."

I snuggled closer. "All right. I'm ready. You ready?"

"Three. Two. One."

He clicked a picture, and it appeared in the text message.

Then, I reached up and typed one word. The only word necessary for the picture before my eyes found Jay again.

"Ready?" I asked.

He smiled. "Ready when you are."

Then, I sent the message. The picture message to both my best friend and my sister. The picture message with only one word that told it all.

ENGAGED!!!

EPILOGUE

KHLOE - TWO MONTHS LATER

I smiled at my engagement ring as the bright winter sunlight captured the radiance of the diamond. In its reflection, a world of glass blanketed with snow, shining for all to see, and reminding me of just how special this time of the year was for us.

For all of us.

"Merry Christmas, beautiful."

I looked up and saw my handsome fiancée handing me a mug of steaming hot apple cider.

"Merry Christmas, Mr. Perfect," I said.

Jay chuckled. "You know damn good and well I'm not perfect."

I shrugged. "You're perfect for me. So, that's all that matters."

He nodded at my ring. "You like it?"

"I love it, Jay. It's… it's completely perfect."

"Like me?"

"Like us."

He wrapped his arm around me as we stood on his back porch. The only footprints in the freshly fallen snow were

Piper's feet as she trudged through the white wilderness. Jay held me tightly against his body as we sipped our cider, enjoying the morning, the beauty of our own White Christmas, the wonderful feeling of having family bursting at the seams in a place that used to hold so much sadness.

That still held sadness sometimes.

"Do you think it'll get easier? You know, with everyone we've lost?" I asked.

Jay kissed the top of my head. "I think it gets easier to accept. But I don't think it ever gets easier, in general."

"Does it bother you?"

"Does what bother me?"

"That I still have love for John?"

"Khlo, look at me."

I lifted my gaze to his and sought comfort in his kind eyes.

"I could never be bothered about something like that," he said.

"Really?" I asked.

"You lost your husband, Khlo. Someone you loved to something no one saw coming. Deaths like that, we never get over. I know that better than anyone."

I nodded slowly. "I suppose you're right."

He kissed my forehead. "Together, we'll get through our grief. We'll cope in healthy ways. And we'll be here to support one another. No matter what."

"Promise?"

"That's a vow I'm willing to take in front of God and everyone else in…"

I sighed. "Don't do it."

He chuckled. "Four months, seventeen days, and nine hours."

I groaned. "You did it."

"Not that I'm counting or anything."

I shook my head as his lips kissed me once more. I leaned against him, watching as Piper jumped around in the natural snow piles that rose above the planes. It felt right, being in Jay's house. Waking up with him every morning. Nestling close to him every night. Sure, we both had our demons, our grief that we carried with us, memories that would always make us cry. But understanding that about one another somehow deepened the connection we had.

Somehow, it made us stronger.

"You know Ollie's going to be upset that he wasn't here to see you give me this ring, right?" I asked.

Jay snickered. "His fault for not coming in last night like he should've."

"Oh, cut him some slack. You know he's been running around like a crazy person lately."

"Oh. Yeah. Right. You blow off a man's leg, and suddenly, he has to be fitted with every kind of prosthetic on the planet."

"I really hope that's your dry wit kicking in."

"Ollie?" Jay asked.

"Well, it's about time I met the man behind the voice," I said as I turned around.

Quinn came around the side of the house. "Can someone help me with his shit? He's packed as if he's staying for two months."

Jay chuckled. "Nice to know some things never change."

"Come here, asshole," Ollie said.

I smiled as they hugged. A big, long, back-clapping hug. I wanted to give the two of them some time for themselves. Though, I was anxious to hear about the man Jay talked about so much. I stepped away from them and followed Quinn, my ring still catching my eye every once in a while.

"It's a beautiful ring," she said.

I smiled. "It's perfect."

"Come on. Everyone grab a bag," Dad said.

I listened to him heave as Mom's body dangled halfway out of the trunk of the car.

"Holy shit, you weren't kidding," I murmured.

"Yeah, Kent lucked out with this one. Running to get us more coffee. I mean, come on. He knew this was happening. He knew what he was leaving us with," Quinn said.

I rolled my eyes. "Come on. Stop being so dramatic, and let's get the man's stuff inside."

With every bag we dropped by the staircase, it made me wonder how well Ollie would navigate up and down the steps, what with his shiny new silver leg and everything. From what Jay told me, the injury was old. Ollie had been without his leg for going on three years now, but the prosthetic was new. And with the research I had done in my spare time, it sometimes took the wearer of a new prosthetic six weeks to adjust to it.

"Ollie! Are you sure you don't want us to set you up in the living room or something?" I called out.

"You talk like I can't get up and down some steps!" the man bellowed.

Before he ran his new leg straight into the corner of the kitchen chair.

"So, was that yes or a no?" I asked.

"Khloe," Dad hissed.

"What? He almost killed himself on a chair. He might take himself out completely falling over the railing," I said.

Ollie pointed at me. "I like this girl. She's got spunk."

I smiled. "I need spunk to deal with him."

Jay furrowed his brow. "Hey, I'm not that bad."

"Come here. I need to give you a hug. I feel like I know you already," Ollie said.

The man enveloped me in a warm bear hug, and I could quickly tell why he and Jay got along so well. They were cut from the same cloth, both warm, inviting, easy to get along with. I felt relaxed in his presence like I did with Jay. I hoped to see more of him as time went on.

"All right, I've got hot coffees for now, and a nice bag of ground coffee for later," Kent said as he came through the front door.

"There he is! Ollie, this is my new partner, Kent," Jay said.

"And my boyfriend," Quinn piped up with pride.

"And my honorary best friend," I said.

Kent paused. "Wait, honorary? Since when?"

I thumbed over my shoulder at Jay. "Since this guy kinda swiped the title away from you."

Kent snickered playfully. "Man. I've been replaced."

Quinn scoffed. "And what am I? Chopped liver? I thought you were my best friend now."

"Well, does that mean I don't have a best friend?" Ollie asked.

"You can be my new best friend," Kent said.

"Yep, chopped fucking liver," Quinn said.

"Sweetheart, language," Mom said softly.

"Oh, you fuckers are really gonna hate me, then," Ollie said.

Laughter rose from all of us as Kent started passing out the coffees.

"Merry Christmas, man," Jay said.

He clapped Ollie's shoulder, and I could've sworn I saw the two men grow teary-eyed.

"Merry Christmas," Ollie said. "And by the way? I'm glad I'm here. I can't wait to see the two of you get married."

I paused. "Wait, you're here until the wedding?"

"I told you he packed way too much for only a couple of weeks!" Quinn exclaimed.

"I packed to stay as long as I'm needed or wanted. But yes. I'll definitely be back for the wedding," Ollie said.

"Actually, I wanted to talk with you about that," Jay said.

I furrowed my brow. "Talk about what?"

"Uh-oh," Quinn said.

"What?" Kent asked.

"If Khloe doesn't know, then it hasn't been approved. That's how this works," Quinn whispered loudly.

"I can hear you," I said.

"What's up?" Ollie asked.

"Well, Khloe and I have been trying to figure out what to do with her home. She's got this great little one-story cottage with a basement on the outskirts of town. It's nestled in the woods. It's quiet. It's really a great place," Jay said.

I heard where he was going with this. "Yeah, but it's terrible to rent out. It's a bit of a drive to get into town. Or to the grocery stores."

"But there's lots of hiking."

"And walkways."

"And running paths."

Ollie grinned. "Are you wanting me to move in? Is that what this is? You're trying to sell me on a house!"

Jay smiled. "All I'm saying is that there's an empty house we don't know what to do with, a town that has helped me through a great deal, and I'm looking at a friend who could use the same kind of healing power I've undergone these past few months."

"Plus, I need someone in it anyway. I'm tired of checking up on the place just to make sure it's okay," I said.

"And it would be a great place for you to finish your recovery. Much better than that dinky old apartment you're staying in."

Ollie nodded slowly. "How much is it to rent the place?"

I shook my head quickly. "Nothing."

"Nothing?" everyone asked in unison.

I giggled as I walked over to Ollie and settled my hand against his arm.

"I don't owe anything on the house. I mean, other than property tax every year. Pay that and the utilities, and we can work out everything else at a later date," I said.

"So, what do you say?" Jay asked.

Ollie puffed out his cheeks. "That's a lot to uh, to take in."

I rubbed his arm. "Well, you've got time to think about it."

"About two and a half months, judging by how much you packed up," Jay said, chuckling.

Ollie snickered. "You guys would be willing to do that for me?"

"Yes," we all said in unison.

Ollie patted his hand against my own. "Jay, you got yourself a good one here."

I smiled. "He knows."

Jay chuckled. "Yeah, I know."

"Does this mean we can bust out celebratory drinks now? Because this coffee could use some peppermint schnapps," Quinn said.

Ollie pointed at my sister. "That sounds wonderful. What do I have to do to get me one of those?"

Jay grinned. "Accept our offer."

Ollie rolled his eyes. "Well, if you're gonna twist my arm like that..."

"Yay!" I exclaimed.

"So, we didn't have to haul all of his stuff inside?" Quinn asked.

Everyone started laughing as Jay and I hugged his best friend tight.

"Merry Christmas, Ollie," I whispered.

The man sniffled. "Merry Christmas, you two."

"Oh, and let me know when you have time to talk later.

You know, about being my best man and everything," Jay said.

"What the fuck? Hell, yeah, I'm gonna be your best man!" Ollie exclaimed.

As my father started gathering up our coffees to turn them into rich, delectable drinks, I felt my heart filling with warmth. With compassion. With love and support. Finally, I felt grounded again, rooted in a reality that suited me instead of a reality that felt like a play I was forced to participate in. I had an adoring fiancée I woke up to every morning, a house full of family on Christmas, and my fiancée's best friend moving into my old house.

"Do you even know how much I love you?" Jay asked.

I smiled up at him as he blanketed me with his arms.

"I love you, too, Jay."

Piper barked, and I reached my hand down to ruffle her head.

"I love you too, beautiful. Don't you worry," I said.

It didn't get any better than this.

The End

Printed in Great Britain
by Amazon